WICKED, BUT SOMETIMES I CALL HER MAMA

Wicked, But Sometimes I Call Her Mama

Brenda and Angel

Library of Congress Control Number:		2009900066
ISBN:	Hardcover	978-1-4415-0125-7
	Softcover	978-1-4415-0124-0

To order additional copies of this book, contact:
Xlibris Corporation
1-888-795-4274
www.Xlibris.com
Orders@Xlibris.com
52967

DEDICATION

This book is in memory of my grandmother. If it had not been for the way she lived her life and treated me, I wouldn't be able to tell this story. Now I can tell myself that, "I love and miss you Mama, through this healing process." My sincerity is great since I was left so little of you. The latter days of your illness I found how harmful and detrimental ignorance can be in a lifetime, causing you to miss out on the best part of your life; "me". I release you from my past hatred mama and now I can go on and live a life I deserve, without regret. Thank God.

ACKNOWLEDGEMENTS

Brenda:

First, giving all honor to my God in Heaven and His amazing Grace. May God continue to anoint me through His will and His way—I thank You.

Wanda Brown, thank you for your creativity and words of spiritual support.

Angel, my angel, thank you. My co-author, my niece, thank you.

Thank you Mrs. Ruby Sanders for your editing services.

Files, my husband, my chauffeur and my partner with a heart of gold, thank you.

Angel:

Thank you Lord God, I pray for the wisdom and strength to always follow You, in Jesus' name, Amen.

Thank you Mommy!

Thank you Aunt Brenda for trusting me enough to ask; "Sure!"

Introduction

Sitting under the tent as the preacher gave her eulogy, I looked over and across the casket my eyes found the face of Mrs. Mauler standing next to her husband, tall and proud. I began thinking of a moment, just a few months prior to my grandmother's death, while sitting on the side of the bed reading, the phone rang. On the other end was the voice of Mrs. Mauler.

Graciously answering the telephone, I said, "Hello?"

"Hello, Rheese?" Sounding as if she wasn't sure who answered the phone.

"Yes this is Rheese."

"This is Elizabeth, Elizabeth Mauler."

"Yes, I know."

"How are you today, Rheese?"

"I'm good and you?"

"I'm also good. The reason I called, I need your help."

"My help?" My voice releasing words with the sound of great curiosity.

"Yes. Honey Mae just called for Jonathan to come and pick her up and carry her out for the day."

Shocked by this information and intrigued, I listened closely.

"Honey knows that Jonathan's eyes are bad and he's actually legally blind in one eye. The last time she insisted on his coming; he did, almost killing himself."

"Killing himself?"

"Yes, he had a serious car accident and we thank God he came out alive."

Surprised because I'd never been told this story, "Well don't worry Mrs. Mauler and rest assured that you can tell Mr. Mauler not to even think about coming out here, putting himself and others at risk. I'll take care of this end."

"Thank you Rheese."

"You're welcome, but there's no need for thanks. I'll talk with you later, okay"

We hung up the phone. I knew why my grandmother called. She was upset with me for telling her no. No, to the fact that she can't always have her way. No, because I would not allow her to call me 'black ass' again and not defend myself. No, because I won't be denied any longer. Respectfully, I declined being disrespected.

When I went into the room to speak with my grandmother about the phone call and ask why she had done such a thing, she only shrugged her shoulders and turned away pouting.

I heard her say in a low but wicked tone, "I wish I could have a cigarette."

I smiled and walked away remembering when she told me a story just a few days before . . . .

The day my grandfather died was one of the worse days of her life, but a few weeks later, a day came along that was worse. She found out she was pregnant, telling me,

"I was a widow, forty years old and my dead husband was not the father." She knew this because they hadn't had a physical relationship in months. "If he had not died when he did, this child would have killed him or he would have killed me."

I asked her, "What happened to the baby?"

"She died after only a few weeks. She was premature. The news of her and who the father was spread faster than when she was born or died. But I didn't give a damn. Folks don't feed me, clothe me or wipe my black ass, so what they say is a waste of air."

"How did Mr. Mauler feel or what did he do?" I asked.

"He sent me on a trip to Jamaica and I was treated like a queen. I stayed for two weeks, all expenses paid. The men on the island loved to see my big ass walking around. They love big behinds. I could care less about them, but I enjoyed the attention. When I got back, Jonathan couldn't do or give me enough, always feeling guilty about his dirty secret with his black mistress and half colored chile. I didn't help him feel any better; I was too busy reaping the benefits."

After telling me this, my grandmother said she was tired and asked me to leave and allow her to get some rest. I left, understanding the extreme control she had over Mr. Mauler and his groveling ways. But what I couldn't understand was her control over me.

CHAPTER 1

"**S**it your black ass down!" she shouted at me across the room. Her vicious words seemed to vibrate my inner being as they whirled around my head. Even the four walls of her well organized kitchen appeared shaken. The kitchen was beautiful, capturing immediate attention with its enchanting mellow yellow color artfully decorating the walls. Positioned sweetly was the classic purity of white appliances, including an automatic dishwasher. The crisp white, well starched window treatment gave its attention to the wind of the summer breeze. This house had all that any of my dreams could hold except for an angry, cursing grandmother.

"I said, sit your got damn black ass down," she screamed once again in my direction.

My cohorts, Gus, Milly and Eric had without notice willingly vacated themselves from our original agreement, 'Stand and endure together.' Everyone was visibly frightened by my grandmother's abrasive and tyrant behavior.

"Yes", I said to myself, *"you are alone"*.

No one dared to uphold my cause or share my sentiments on being brave. Graciously, the cowards took a seat, obeying the words she had addressed toward us with a malicious tone. Even her precious Persian cat had lack of courage and sprinted out of the room. To the commanding boom of her thunderous voice that echoed and etched negative impressions deep and firmly across our young minds forever, I wanted to yield.

I unequivocally hated my grandmother. I, declared within myself, there would be no orders taken by me from someone I didn't know and someone that didn't know a thing about me. She was a stranger—a total stranger that would doom her only grandchild's first visit to be the last.

Being a child, with a child's heart and with a child's imagination, I linked protection, comfort and security with grandmothers, but found no such connection of safety with this lady.

"Who was she? Why the entity of her in my life?" I affiliated nothing between us but distance.

Only six or seven years of age at the time, I embedded my senses with standing tall and consumed myself with the destructive desire to challenge, defeat and extinguish the blaze of lady Godzilla.

Driven by an unseen force that guided me from a course of safety straight to the pits of hell, I was relentless. Her intimidating wrath was great but no longer was it greater than my hurt now turned to anger stemming from her severe absence of love.

"What did I have that she didn't like? Was it my life, my skin color?" Once again, she introduced me to her infamous words.

"Sit your got damn, ugly, black ass down," she said insisting on my having a seat.

Her eyes were like heat seeking missiles searching to connect with mine. I wanted to seek refuge. I began glancing in all directions in order not to have eye contact.

"Please, God help me to defuse this ugly situation." I quickly prayed.

I guess God did not hear my prayer. Things only became worse. Slowly losing the little independence remaining for me in this impossible and detrimental standoff, I still didn't move. Oh how I wanted to move. All eyes were focused on the two of us, heads dancing back and forth like spectators at a World Cup Tennis tournament. Like faithful fans, they held their breaths waiting for the last volley of the ball.

Honey Mae, my grandmother, a lady I sometimes call mama, entertained everyone in the room except me with her colorful and vivid usage of curse words. Suddenly I saw and heard soft giggles in the background, laughing at what they found humorous. While on the other hand, I intrigued them as they watched with horrific anticipation of my absolute defiance. No one knew how desperately I struggled to set myself free from being snared in her web, knowing in the end there was no trophy for me. With her, there was no letting go, especially since I placed myself in this ungodly forsaken situation.

"Oh God, here I come again." Praying, *"How do I decrease her anger and heighten her awareness of my craving for submission to her alarming command of sitting my black behind down?"*

No matter the cruelty of her expressions to my tender ears, I honestly wanted to sit down. Desperately seeking a way out of this problem, hoping it would vanish and be eliminated. I felt my insides tremor.

"Oh God, I'm only a child, help me."

Please tell me why my body was continuing to allow my mind to stand it up? Before this Hell began, I remembered that . . .

The morning began as a good day. A captivating sunshine, the air was filled with fragrances of magnolia and honeysuckle. Hummingbirds' continuous movement embarked and drank the summers' sweet nectar. Mama had lavishly prepared a festive breakfast fit for kings and queens.

All the way from the bedroom, I could taste the flavor of the hickory smoked bacon, floating from the kitchen. Accompanied by eggs, grits, fried potatoes and homemade biscuits, adorned with hot melted butter and drizzled with honey. I had never been served food on beautifully decorated china and eaten it with silver stemware. Before my first bite, my tongue salivated. Sadly such a great meal would be tarnished by a very disastrous encounter of disagreement.

After breakfast, we cleaned the kitchen harmoniously, even to mama's high standards. She had then given us permission to carry our harmony out with us to play, but warned us not to eat any green plums growing on the vine.

"Forbidden fruit in a field of temptation," I thought.

Combined with Alabama's humidity, we became drunk with fun and games. Refueling ourselves with mama's extra special homemade lemonade, we embraced childhood. Nature became our background singers carrying on with much chatter and having its own way of showing us, we were all invited to its open doors of entertainment and hospitality. Unfairly taunting us with a seductive lure, nature caused our young minds to travel to just a few steps away; a few steps that would escort us to the prohibited green plums.

Our appetites still suppressed from a filling breakfast and the music of lemonade sloshing around in our bellies couldn't stop our minds from tracing an outline of mischievous thoughts. Like the humming bird after dancing around the bloom, we wanted to taste its beverage.

Never before had Gus, Milly and I ever been forbidden to eat of the fruit, red yellow or green. We came armed, loaded with palms filled with salt. The only stop sign was a stomach ache and the only consequence was not to complain. We as children did not have the full understanding of our hands being barred from the fruit that weighed heavy in our coming conclusion of breaking mama's rule and eating from the bush anyway.

Immediately after indulging, somehow mama learned of our youthful disobedience and called us to come inside. Each one of us having a finger to point at the other, finding someone to place the blame upon, no one wanted ownership. One thing for sure, we were all afraid.

After we were summonsed, we began discussing in low-toned voices, our plot to deceive. Knowing the deep trouble that laid in wait as we slowly marched our way back to the house, we decided to stand together. Our steps drew us closer to the house, when suddenly I heard sniffles from the background. I turned to see Eric wiping beneath his nose with his forearm. This was truly a signal I was losing troop. Our first coalition was damned; our first coalition fell apart. Each, now supporting our own heaviness of fear, drew closer to the lady standing in the back doorway; lady Godzilla.

I looked up and was caught by her stare, which seemed to dominate and paralyze my movement like snake venom. No one stopped walking but me. Once released from the trance, I had to run in order to catch up as the others climbed the stairs. Mama gave each one of us a swat with her large wooden spoon, as we filed past her, promising more to follow.

The last to receive my strike was when I made my declaration within, *"More licks for them, but no more for me."*

I wasn't going to be punished with harshness for such a ridiculous crime. She had no right to beat on me for any reason. If she couldn't love me, she surely couldn't beat me. The only one she had a right to enforce her rules upon was Eric.

He belonged to her.

He was her half white child of whom she had guardianship over; Eric was the child that filled her days and her nights with joy and happiness. Something I could never seem to do, no matter how hard I struggled to convey to her, I wanted her love.

If eating freely the foods applied from God through His finger of love could cause division, I was willing to accept the broken wings of any bond between me and my grandmother, but I was not going to accept the beating.

Seeing Gus, Milly and Eric, my cohorts, begin to weep, I laughed in the face of my first coalition; laughing because it lasted as long as a slave on his way to the poll to vote. It was dead just like the slave.

I had no concept of how great the distance between my grandmother and I was until her words began that day, like the hot blade of a sword melting through butter.

Again she bellowed, "Fool, you're moving like you got molasses stuck up your ass. You better sit your sorry black ass down before I come over there and knock the hell out of you."

Reacting as if she was speaking to them, from the corner of my eye, I could see my force gradually disengaging from me. Eric, Milly and Gus repositioned themselves erect in the chairs where they sat, pouring confirmation of treachery in my open wound of being alone. Enflamed with anger, I watched betrayal unfold before my very eyes. I silently stood still inhaling and exhaling with deep hard breaths and fists clenched. I was anticipating nothing short of merciless death to be my companion.

Gus, Milly and Eric began waiting for the culmination of music from this drama to commence playing as events began to swell to a possible fatal conclusion. The music never happened and the conclusion eventually arrived.

Clenching her teeth while speaking and pointing at the chair where I stood, she said once again, "Sit down got damn it!"

She gestured with body motions as if she were coming around the table to give introduction of her fist to my face but stopped as I began to ease down into the chair.

Believing every word that she uttered from her mouth, I tried to hold back the tears that presented themselves. Traveling rapidly down my small and narrow face, the tears captured my emotions. Embarrassed, I'd succumbed to her violent demand.

My hatred grew deeper for her, especially her calling me so many black names. If no one else knew how dark my skin complexion was, I knew. I saw myself in the mirror everyday. I looked at her with much disdain and malice and I didn't care if she noticed or further threatened my life.

Once I was seated, everyone seemed to give a sigh of relief. This must have met the approval of mama also, because she quickly vacated the room, giving me illusions to believe the debt was paid and the account was settled.

Needing to recover from my humiliation, I got up from my chair began flexing my muscles, shaking my butt and making funny facial expressions, trying to make the others laugh at my behavior. Placing my thumbs in my ears while wiggling my fingers and sticking out my tongue, I sang a made up song, "♫Neh na na na na na na, I don't need you for me♫." Wiggling my tongue with more vigor, I didn't know how much I would need them.

If only I had taken heed to Milly's efforts of trying to warn me of my soon surprise attack as they watched my disobedience, they were also watching my grandmother watch me. Protecting themselves, they never moved a muscle, except for Milly's constant eye movement trying to signal me of mama's presence, I couldn't recognize the attempted rescue because I was too busy being the center of attention. I felt as if I held the victory, a winning that was short lived with serious consequences.

She stood behind me with her weapon of choice, a switch braided from parts of the old oak tree found in her backyard. She struck me from behind with a wind whistling strike landing across my shoulders. Frightened by the hit, I forgot I was entertaining.

All I could hear was mama's continuous ranting. "I told you one too many times to sit your ugly black ass down. You must have a got damn death wish, making you not want to live and not believing crap stinks."

Unleashing another blow as I ran around the table, she said, "You're so grown and want to do like you want, you can, but not in my got damn house. I have more butt whuppings to put on you than your little black ass can hold."

I started running through the house with her hot on my heels. She wasn't as easy to shake off my trail as I had once thought. She was bringing more and more strikes that never seemed to have an ending. We were both yelling so loud; however, mine was for a plea of help. Neighbors thought a murder was being committed and they were possibly right.

The more I yelled the more licks were unleashed. She finally stopped her relentless terror after the sound of a rhythmic rapping came upon the door. I'll never forget or stop being grateful to the man that was positioned in the front screen door, standing on a pair of crutches and missing one of his legs.

Mama looked at him and smiled but not before she made me one last promise, "Next time I tell you to do something got damn it, you better do it the second it comes out of my got damn mouth onto your sorry black ass ears; three strikes on my team is the hell out."

I looked as he stood there in the doorway and noticed he wasn't the best looking man, but his presence and his timing were beautiful. I thanked God for this attention breaker. Mama walked over and unlatched the screen door and opened it wide for her gentleman caller and at the same time said, "All of you go outside before I lose my damn mind!"

Everyone, including me, moved so fast we almost knocked each other down. When we reached outside, Gus and Milly raced for the glider and Eric jumped into the rocking chair. It really drew no concern to me as to where I was going to sit, I only wanted to sit somewhere to nurse my welts and wipe away my tears.

I remember sitting on my worn out behind and holding hostage the thought of somehow killing my grandmother.

Wondering, *"where is my mama Flora?"*

One child dark and one child of light skin color, but Mama Flora desperately loved them both. *"Where is my big mama?"*

I contemplated never being able to call out to her in excitement or jest, never being able to throw my wide open arms around her large body and broad shoulders. She was so big, my tiny hands couldn't meet and clasp behind her, but she knew the greatness of my love.

Big Mama's and Mama Flora should always smell of baked sweet potatoes, causing my appetite to have a mind of its own. My Big Mama's aprons should be dusted with flour and the dress should be made from the bag which the flour came from, while she would be standing there sweating profusely as she pulled out of the pot bellied stove, her famous homemade tea cakes. Seeing the big bright smile come upon my face, she sprinkled them with extra sugar. Limping on her worn knees that have to struggle to carry all of the extra weight her body had gained, she would never grow tired, never too tired to share a piping hot cookie with the grandchild she loved, me. To curse me wouldn't be a question.

"Please, someone tell me where is my Big Mama? I need to tell her that I love her, but most of all I need to hear that she loves me too."

Even when I hate my grandmother the most, at the same time I'm thinking how beautiful she looks. If beauty were held for riches, her wealth would have a countless end and I would be heir of great inheritance.

That day, she was dressed in a green, pencil slim, cotton, form fitting, sundress. The dress allowed you to become acquainted with her shapely figure; it defined every curve her body possessed, also accentuating her flawlessly bowed legs that glided down into her matching four inch stiletto heels. Her hair was neatly placed in a French roll upsweep and her neck and ears were graced by beautiful fresh water pearls. No matter how she mistreated me, strangely enough I dismissed and admired, wanting someday to be like her.

I wanted beauty, clothes, money, purses, shoes, a car, nice home and modern appliances. I wanted everything that she did have and we didn't; no matter how hard my mother struggled we didn't have.

I remember my father, my grandmother's son, did not marry my mother and when he died I was about three or four years old. My mother tried to get social security after his death for me but my grandmother intervened. I did not get his social security because my grandmother declared I was not his child. I heard her once telling someone that I was too black and ugly to be a part of her, or maybe she was wrong; maybe she was too mean to be a part of me.

Rudely, I was removed from my thoughts as Eric exclaimed, "Let's play dodge ball!"

Still feeling the burn from my welts while Gus and Milly jumped up with excitement I continued to sit on the steps. Eric said to me again, "Let's play dodge ball."

Looking at him with contempt and between sniffles, I said, "I don't want to play ball."

"Awww, come on." Milly insisted.

"Leave me alone, I don't want to play."

Annoyed with my persistent selfish behavior, my brother Gus jumped up in my face pointing his finger, and said, "Ok, we'll leave you alone. Anyway, you're just mad because you just got your butt beat."

"So!" I cleverly responded.

"So, is right. Your butt is so'." Gus said as everyone started to laugh, causing my tears to renew their flow.

I was angry. "I don't need you guys anyway," I told them, "and I'm going home."

"Sure you are. So go ahead." Gus dared me.

"Watch me."

I turned to go inside the house and to my surprise I ran straight into the face of lady Godzilla. She was once again standing in the doorway. I thought I had peed in my pants, I knew if she had not killed me before, now I surely would be dead. My body couldn't stand to be hit another lick.

I said in a low whisper, "Help me God."

I couldn't move, I was frozen, never once did I think that she would be standing there. I was disappointed because I thought she was too busy entertaining to worry herself about me or the others while we were out playing. How wrong I was.

While checking on us, Mr. Prentice sat quietly at the kitchen table, patiently waiting for mama's return. I wondered how much she had heard. When she asked me, "Did I hear you say that you were going home?" She answered my question, she had heard enough.

Scared stiff, I began stumbling over my words, "Uh, uh, ye . . . uh yes, yes ma'am."

I knew it would be against my health to lie now since she heard every word I said. If I could lie and get away with it, I figured this would be the right time, but I knew I couldn't. As she opened up the screen door and invited me to come inside, my reluctance grew and once again her eyes pierced my soul . . . .

"You know what?" Her voice more gentle but cross. "Bring your little black ass in here and get your raggedy stuff, so you can go home, it's ok by me."

Everyone was stunned but I was suffocating. As Mama flicked me a phony grin, my pride was shattered. I wanted to tell her I was just joking, I didn't mean it, but I knew she would not be listening. I was surprised she didn't snatch and beat me down as I approached where she stood.

Instead she said, "Pick up your pace, come on, so you can go."

As I was walking slowly and quite nervous, she said, "Hurry so you won't let the flies come inside."

Quickly moving past her, I went straight into the bedroom and gathered my things, realizing my mouth had written a check my behind couldn't cash.

"Please God!" I wanted to cry out; I wanted to stay—not to stay around mama or at her house, but to stay with my brother and Milly. It really didn't matter if I was around Eric or not, the jury was still out reaching a verdict on how I really felt about him. Eric was Aunt Lucille's grandson, and Lucille was my grandmother's baby sister.

Aunt Lucille's daughter Queen gave birth to Eric after Aunt Lucille's death. Queen was only sixteen years of age when she gave birth to him. Soon after, she moved to Brooklyn, New York, leaving Eric behind with my grandmother.

No one ever knew Eric's father. We knew he had to have one, but no one ever knew of him. The only thing people figured out about his dad was that he had to be a white man because of the white features Eric carried, golden, curly hair, thin lips and skin with a slight golden tan.

Unlike me, my skin was dark as a Maui night; my jet black hair was so nappy, it played different tunes whenever my mother tried to comb through it. The closest thing I have on me to being bright enough for my grandmother to love me was my teeth.

I should feel sorry for Eric since he was abandoned by his father and he had no immediate family, but I can't, because he is taking over my life leaving me feeling alone and abandoned. Eric lived a charmed life; in reality, he lived my life.

My grandmother continued to stand in the doorway as I gathered and put my few pieces of clothes in a brown paper bag. When I finished, I turned and headed for the door. Once again she opened the door, this time for my exit. She had become my personal valet. She didn't say another word and I lowered my head as I passed her.

Milly, Gus and Eric were still on the porch, true cowards they were, never saying a word or leaving their seats. Possibly, the offenders stuck around wanting to see everything that would happen, seeing if I would live or die. The only thing that took place was my leaving.

By now, it was noonday and it only took a few minutes before the sun pierced through my mane, sizzling my scalp. Walking home in this heat and humidity could cause anyone delayed breathing. As I began my walk I searched for any shaded area I could find to give me comfort. I started the long walk home and I didn't look back. I had begun with a slow pace but suddenly my legs started to pick up speed without my permission soon causing me to begin running, and running I did.

The faster I ran, the more I smiled because I was going home. There, I would find some consolation, I would not be constantly reminded of how black and ugly I was. Things at home were better, but sometimes the same as it was at my grandmother's house. I knew my mother loved me, but I felt inferior to my brother.

Having different fathers, my brother inherited his half Indian father's complexion, giving him an advantage in a light, bright world. However, today when I get home I could feel safe; I would feel as though I did not have to compete.

When I arrived home, my mother was surprised and shocked to see me running up the long flight of concrete steps leading to the porch where she was sitting. She gave me a few minutes to catch my breath, then I told her of my ordeal, she had no sympathy, she showed no concern, without saying a word she got up from her chair and began hitting me on my behind with her hand and told me I had to go back.

With added trauma to my already sore behind, my world shattered as I heard my mother say, "Get your stuff and go back over to Miss Honey Mae's right now."

Before I knew it, I yelled, "NO!"

Looking at me with much surprise, her eyes bulged resembling my grandmother. She said, "Little girl, who do you think you're talking to?"

Feeling complete remorse and my face cascaded with tears I said, "I'm sorry mama but you don't understand she called me all kinds of bad names."

Pointing her finger in the direction that lead to my grandmother's house, she was ordering me to leave without saying a word.

Walking down the stairs, I heard her say the old cliché, "Sticks and stones will break your bones, but names will never hurt you."

I turned, looked at my mother and I said, "Oh but how words do hurt."

Head hung down I joined into another journey with the sweltering heat walking back to my grandmother's house. I thought to myself, "*Lord help me, because the last thing I needed was to receive a tan*". At that moment I felt no love, no hugs, no kisses, all I felt was, alone.

Then I quickly changed my mind and I started to pray, "*Dear God, if you allow my skin to tan maybe I'll become so dark I'll become invisible. Then no one would find me. No one would have to love me, then no one would have to care.*"

Topping the hill that lead to my grandmother's house, I could see Gus, Milly and Eric playing under the large tree in the front yard. When they finally looked up and saw me coming, they ran toward me, Gus cried out, "We knew you would be back."

Shocked, I asked, "How?"

"Your grandmother told us you would be coming back."

"How did she know?" I asked with much curiosity.

Eric answered in a strange tone, "Because she's mama."

That very moment I wondered if I really wanted Eric's life. After sensing my pain, they gathered around me. No one teased me, no one said another word about that day; we just began to play and we reformed our coalition.

CHAPTER 2

About thirty minutes later, mama called in the troop to have supper, I was hoping this call included me. She didn't seem surprised to see me coming inside with the others and I would normally have tried to be first to enter, especially for food, but last place seemed to suit me quite well today.

While heading toward the door I prayed, *"Dear God, please don't let her send me away, I have nowhere else to go, not even home."*

Dying of thirst, I was hot, starving and exhausted. I displayed the lowest of rank I could muster up in humbleness, whatever she was cooking in the kitchen smelled so good that crawling and licking her floor to a sparkling clean for the crumbs at this time was not beneath me.

When we reached the kitchen, I saw there were four place settings, always allowing us as children to eat first, never eating with us and the one-legged man gone, I assumed and hoped that the fourth setting still meant that I was included. So I prayed again, *"please God, let her same routine stand right now."* He heard my prayer, my prayer was answered, I was allowed to eat.

Noticeably she had changed clothes, changed into a very casual yellow outfit consisting of petal pushers and a matching cotton blouse. The mid-calf pants, hugged her legs like a hand in glove. Walking around in bare feet could not diminish her level of class or subtract from her grace and beauty.

The table was set with great food. I went straight for the juggler, pulling the chair from underneath the table I was ready to dive in.

Her words grabbed my ears that came barely over a whisper, yet strong and firm. She said, "No! Go and wash those nasty little hands of yours."

I thought, *"Last one in, first to mess up."* I guess the sun had baked my brain because I knew never to sit at the table and eat without washing my hands.

Embarrassed, humiliated and ravenous, I said, "I'm sorry." I released the back of the chair as quickly as I touched it.

I said to myself, *"Now, you want to sit your butt down."*

I walked briskly toward the bathroom with my head hung down, I wanted to die.

I looked up long enough to see her gaze upon me as she stood, leaning against the kitchen counter, a cigarette between her fingers and legs crossed at the ankle. For some unknown reason to me, this visual picture of my grandmother has forever been in my mind.

When we came back to the table and grace was said, I remember seeing my grandmother filtering her fingers through the hundreds of golden, curly locks of Eric's hair, picking unwanted bits of grass and weeds protruding from his mane which he had gathered during the course of our playtime.

When she became aware of my looking, she gave a cryptic smirk aimed just for my eyes and my eyes only. I did the best thing that I could without showing disgust and dislike and not wanting my food to be taken away, I just lowered my head back down, wishing that she would come and play through my hair, which could not easily be done, since my kinky hair would cause her to stop too many times. Maybe she could just come over and touch it or maybe she could just sit down and play footsies under the table with me, or maybe she could tickle me after a round of itsy bitsy spider, anything resembling love, anything that would leave me with a memory of a gentle touch from her. Wishing was all I had along with nappy hair and dark skin.

After the last stem of grass was pulled from Eric's hair, she poured up a glass of something she called 'rot-gut,' short for, Joe Louis Whiskey. She took a sip from her glass, lit the cigarette from the stove, she proceeded outside to relax in the wrought iron glider on the front porch where a welcomed breeze was always available even when weather was hot and the humidity was high. This well kept, high maintenance grandmother of mine, was a bootlegger, whiskey making, .38 caliber pistol packing, cursing, man using, high-spirited, fashion-plate of a lady that didn't give a damn about no one except Eric.

After dinner she allowed us to go out and play just a little while longer then called us in, gave us a bath and we went to bed. The next morning, bright and early, breakfast was prepared for us and as usual it was great. Afterwards, we headed for home. Gus, Milly and I skipped along down the hillside that lead us off mama's property unto the hot, tar paved street that the black community had recently inherited.

As black children we had come a long way from the rocky dirt roads that had twisted ankles, battered bare feet, and skinned knees from learning to ride bikes and roller skating. The new paved streets were welcomed and more pleasurable for children to adapt at play. I began running home with gladness as Gus and Milly lagged behind, because I knew, this time my mother wouldn't send me back.

Turning around to wave my final goodbye's I noticed mama's arms were draped around Eric as she stood behind him. I quickly lowered my hands and tucked my feelings deep down inside of myself hidden in a dark place—a place my grandmother had created for me inside my heart. I had all this sadness in my life because of the darkness of my complexion.

I always told myself, "*It was ok.*"

From that day, I never spent another night or day as a child with my grandmother. I continued my life as usual without her. Never celebrating birthdays, no tree trimming at Christmas, no opening gifts, no new clothes, shoes or toys bought just for me.

Many years passed, many years lost between us. She willingly shared all those things and years with Eric. Verdict in, and confirmed, I hate Eric also.

I remembered one day when I was older while looking through my grandmother's old photos that captured many smiles, hugs and kisses from family members and friends being exchanged, but I realized, most of the people I didn't recognize and they would not recognize me, possibly they had never heard of me. This made something very wrong with all the pictures; there was no image of me although Eric was present and accounted for on each and every one; making him my replacement. He sat under Christmas trees, opening gifts, receiving hugs and kisses from my grandmother, playing with his new toys. Also gathered around him were many familiar faces he seemingly knew and they knew him as well.

There was one picture in particular that stood out from the rest; a picture of my father, balancing the toddler on the top of his new car. I envied that photo, a very emotional Kodak moment for me to see, because I will never have the good fortune to share something so special with him. He met his demise before my fourth birthday.

"*If he had lived*", I ask myself, "*would he spend his time with me? Would his presence help mama to love me? Would he lift me onto the top of his car? Would mama have never called me bad black names? Would I ever have started putting bleach in my bath water, or using bleaching cream I stole from the corner store in order to lighten my skin? Would I no longer hate myself?*"

All because of my color, I was teased at play, school and church, teased by family, friends, strangers and worst of all, my grandmother. I could never get away from my shameful color or my ugly features, not even in my dreams.

Introduced to racism at an early age, not from protesters of the Alabama bus boycott or the March in Selma, not even at the Woolworth lunch counter, or the KKK, no Bull Connor, Jim Crow or the George Wallace's of the world. No 16th Street church bombing, fire hoses filled with skin ripping water or vicious dogs unmuzzled and unleashed guided to attack the innocent, I didn't even know about racism as peaceful marchers such as Martin Luther King Jr., Shuttleworth or Abernathy, sacrificing their safety for my freedom or Malcolm X's leadership by any means necessary. No, I learned not racism from these circumstances, I learned in the midst of my very own family.

When I was old enough and had the ability to understand the impact of Martin Luther King Jr. and his heart wrenching 'I Have a Dream' speech spoken from the Lincoln Center, addressing thousands reaching as far back as the Washington Monument, I was having dreams of my own. I dreamed never to one day be called black gal or juju baby, darkie, tar baby, spot, ink mark, soot, smoky, navy, ace of spades, sambo, dark shadow, ghost and many others not to mention the least of my favorite, the one that I hated the most, black ass, famously given by my grandmother.

Martin Luther King Jr. fought for equality for people; I fought to have equality from people. Racism flashed signs displaying words like, 'For Whites Only', hanging over fountains, restroom doors or barstools. But my grandmother's racism hung in her heart for me and in her eyes and mouth came flowing, 'For Light Skin Only'.

Skin color has always plagued me, taunted daily by a boy named Wally Harkmon. He was an ugly boy, with an ugly name. He was the ugliest boy found in all the adjacent communities, but being ugly didn't overshadow my darkness. His jokes always overpowered mine.

Once, a short lived soda came out on the market called, "white lightning." The theme consisted of these words, "White lightning, tastes so good it's frightening." Kids I grew up with, when I ask, never seem to remember the soda or the theme, but the kids I grew up with, when I ask if they remember the song Wally Harkmon made up, they can remember bits and pieces, if not all of Wally's magical words from that jingle addressing my dark complexion. "Black lightening, she so black she could be whitening."

With a healthy dose of our childhood friends' laughter gave momentum to his ignorance and to my pain. However, the song became a hit and was sung quite often. His warped version of this song and sense of humor hurt me more and deeper than any knives could cut. These cruel words rang over and over in my head giving a lifetime of unhappiness, like unwanted pipe music when stuck on an elevator.

I was constantly being reminded that my dark skin was an ugly curse, no matter how many pretty clothes were bought for me to wear; clothes could never make people see past my unbleached skin. I bedded down each night with self pity, contemplating suicide as a daily friend.

This was a scary thing for me as a child, believing death would be the only way to help me escape from what was thought to be living hell.

There was only so much my mother could do to protect me from the Wally Harkmons of the world and all of the neighboring bullies, most importantly how could she save me from my grandmother, or how could she save me from myself? Oh how I wanted my grandmother to die. How I wanted to die myself.

Hate for the both of us grew inside me everyday.

CHAPTER 3

Forty plus years had passed since the day of our dreadful encounter, that I nailed the coffin shut on our already crippled relationship—a relationship I thought was dead forever.

It was an early morning in July and it was already smoldering with the beginnings of unbearable heat. The heat index was in the triple digits. With Alabama's humidity, the weather could be brutal.

Being the sole care giver of my grandmother, I started finding it difficult to keep up with the days of the week. It really didn't matter because all days seemed to blend in and to be the same. Whatever the day I was grateful unto God for another one.

Awake since 4 a.m., I just laid there in bed and listened to the rhythm of the half baked job done on the wobbling ceiling fan as it rapidly turned. Looking over on the nightstand, I glanced at the clock and the bright red numbers displayed 4:22 a.m. and only twenty two minutes had passed since I last checked the time. It seemed like hours. I could feel that the fan was no longer giving off a cool breeze; its comfort level had been discontinued.

Not yet ready to get out of bed and start the day, I just lay there. The light of dawn had finally made its way in through the window, resting on my pillow loving me once again. I love the warmth of its touch, kissing my face and remaining my silent bedfellow. The time on the clock display now read 5:00 a.m. Suddenly the music from the alarm starts to blare out the voice of the great Shirley Ceasar. The voice came in strong, sending chills down my spine and tears on my cheeks as she sang ♫ "For the nine months I carried you, growing inside me, no charge. For the nights I sat up with you, doctored you, prayed for you, no charge." ♫

Wiping away tears and sweat, I couldn't tell the difference, I got up and sat on the side of the bed, thanking God for this moment in a new day and prayed that 'today' I do something to please and serve Him.

I slipped my feet inside my favorite worn bunny slippers, one shoe missing an ear. I love them, even if they won't come clean any longer. The more people promise to buy me a new pair if I throw them away, the more I love them. Besides I have new slippers, with the price tags still attached, but somehow bunny will stay.

Soon an aroma began to tickle my nose and tap on my thoughts. The fresh fragrance of a brewing pot of coffee seem to have overwhelming power, reminding me why I have fallen in love with my maid, "the automatic coffee maker," the same love that I have for my bunny slippers.

Before heading to the kitchen I got up, went over and turned on the window unit air-conditioner. I stood there in front of it allowing it to blow through my oversized t-shirt. Oh, how good it felt as my body, feeling like a ball of heat rolling with sweat, accepted the air helping me to quickly cool down.

The nipples on my breast saluted and stood at attention. They knew and recognized great pleasure instantly. With the dawn caressing my face, kissing my cheeks and the air-conditioner giving me such joy with its cooling sensations to my body, I decided, I didn't need my husband after all. As far as I was concerned he could continue with his divorce procedures and I wouldn't be mad at him.

It's funny how little you need in life as years pass. Quietly walking away from my satisfying thoughts, I went into the bedroom of my grandmother. Finding her still asleep, I smiled, I did not want to disturb her peaceful rest. She had grown very old and so fragile.

Tipping across the floor, I had become anxious to pour my first cup of 'java', as mama would always say, "I like my coffee black, no cream no sugar, just like a man, the best way to drink your coffee." I wondered if she could have just considered me a cup of coffee when I was little; then she could have loved me. With my favorite mug filled with coffee, my thin floral robe and bunny slippers, I headed outside. All I needed was a cigarette, if I smoked to climax a good and thrilling morning. *"Sorry Lord."*

As I climbed onto the glider that looked like the one mama had when I was a kid, but it wasn't, I took a sip of beverage, relaxed and sipped some more. Indulging myself and glad to be in God's presence, I said, "Thank You Lord," when out of the blue a wild rabbit appeared from the wooded area behind mama's house. Watching the bunny explore his newly discovered adventure, I became intrigued.

I stretched out on the cushioned glider and I started to drift slowly to sleep. The last thing I remembered was looking up at God's masterpieces of artwork and thinking that it was forever changing its beauty; I love looking at the clouds. Clicking my heels together, I said, *"I must be in Emerald City Toto"*.

At the very moment God blew His breath and sent a very welcomed breeze that caressed my face, I closed my eyes in appreciation. When I opened my eyes, the bunny was still hopping, sniffing and nibbling his way to his own happiness. One thing for sure, we were both enjoying a beautiful morning together.

I don't remember when I fell asleep, but was awakened by the sting of a mosquito, causing me to slap my face really hard. A little dazed, immediately I looked down at my watch, hoping the time I was looking at was wrong. I squeezed my eyes tightly then opened them looking at my watch again. Minutes had turned into an hour.

Looking across the lawn for the bunny and finding he wasn't there, I guess he had completed his mission and vanished back into the woods. I jumped up still slightly disoriented; my feet somehow had become tangled in my robe, causing me to stumble. Gathering my composure, I ran quickly inside. I don't remember opening the door. I just remember being in the house.

My heart felt as if it would come out of my body and plant itself on the outside of my chest. Adrenalin flowing, heart pounding, I ran energetically through the house, hurdling over any and all obstacles in my path until I reached mama's bedroom. There were only a few seconds from the porch to mama's room, but it seemed longer and my mind carried so many thoughts.

In spite of all the noise I brought inside with me, she was still asleep. I released a deep breath and a great sigh of relief. I walked over to the window and let up the shades because she loved the sunshine. She would always tell me that the sunshine means; "A new day to do it right or to get it wrong. I've had so many damn wrong days, I think today I'll do it right."

Looking down on her, she looked so calm in the hospital bed that Hospice had supplied for the assistance with her care, a bed she didn't want, but they felt she needed. Standing there for a minute I thought she seemed a little too calm for me, so I placed my hand under her nose to see if she was still with me. Feeling the air from her nostrils, I knew she was still here. I exhaled.

"Where is all the fight she always had?

Where did the hell-raising, foul mouth, non-caring attitude go?

Does it go and sit on a shelf and wait for her health to return?

Or does it attach itself to someone else as it escapes from one body to another?"

As I continued to look at her my heart felt heavy, I gently shook her while calling her name.

"Mama, wake up."

Pausing before I called her name again. "Mama, wake up," still no response. I became alarmed. *"I felt the air under her nostrils or did I?"* I questioned myself.

"Mama, wake up, it's me!" I said louder with a little more aggressiveness.

Slowly opening her eyes, she gave that very pretentious smile she always gives when she is annoyed.

"I know who the hell you are with all that damn hollering, I'm sick not deaf." *Oh yes, she's alright. Maybe all the fight isn't gone, just weak.* I walked over and turned on her window unit.

"Ready for your bath ol' girl?" I asked her.

Once, her voice was very loud and strong, now it was lower, but still somewhat strong.

"No, I'm not ready for a bath. Now take your happy ass somewhere and sit down."

"It's always no, give me something else."

"Hell no," she replied smugly. "How's that?"

"So when will you be ready?"

"I'll tell you later."

"Tell me now."

"I wish you would let me sleep damn it." She said, as only mama could.

"Wishing won't change the fact. You'll get a bath and I'm not going anywhere until you get cleaned up."

"Maybe if I throw in a few more damns and a couple of black asses, you'll be happy and leave me alone."

Breathing for her was difficult; she took deep breaths with almost every word she spoke.

"You want to bathe me everyday. When I was using my cat for sex, I had a reason to wash it everyday. Now it's retired, so I don't need a bath. I ain't using it."

"Look lady, let's not fight about this again. You know I'll win and you know I'm going to give you your bath, so let it be." I told her with less patience.

"You must be trying to wash all the damn black off me. Just leave some black on me. That's all I ask you to do," she said while coughing uncontrollably, leaving her where she couldn't say another word at that moment. The coughing was getting worse by the day. She waved her hand, dismissing me and I walked out of the room. Her coughs soon subsided.

When I came back into the room with her pail of water and soap, she said, "As I was trying to say before I was interrupted by those damn coughs," was almost choking as she tried to fight back the cough again, "Leave some black on my damn ass, so when I die, people will know who I am in my casket, especially those church asses."

"I'll leave a little black on you mama and when you need a casket, no time soon of course, people will know you regardless. Trust me on this. If you were to turn white, people will know you."

She laughed out loud, coughing in between. Showing all thirty-two gums. She was no longer able to wear her dentures, due to the tremendous amount of weight she had lost; she went from a twenty to a six in dress size. She had become nothing but wrinkled skin and bones.

She made me promise to put in her dentures on her home going day saying, "Whether Heaven or Hell, I'm taking my teeth with me, I paid for them." All she could think about were those stupid teeth not what to put on her body, just what to put in her mouth. I guess she was thinking pearly whites instead of pearly gates. Heaven, help my grandmother.

I find myself feeling sorry for her especially since no one seems to ever visit or call except for my mother and a friend of mine checking in on me. They would sometimes make their way into my grandmother's room for a visit and short conversation. This always seemed to lift her spirits.

Mama had alienated all her friends, even her only living sibling, her sister Mabel. Aunt Mabel never called because mama severed those ties long ago.

This is the same woman that didn't want to have anything to do with me in or outside of this house, when I was a child. She didn't want anything to do with the darkness of my skin. Now, I was an adult, residing inside the house that as a child I wasn't allowed. Now she is the child and I am the one to do everything for her, to take care of her because she can't do it for herself.

This house use to seem bigger when I was small, but now I seem too big for the small wood framed house. It doesn't seem as special as I remember; in fact, now, it resembles a shack. *I was an heir to a shack.*

Finishing with her bath, I changed the linen and wrestled with her making sure she swallowed her medicine. With sweat pouring down my face, I took a seat trying to cool down. I seem to have to fight with her about everything. She no longer wanted to eat. The nurse said she would be fine as long as she continued to take in fluids, but I still worried.

Exhausted sometimes from being a caregiver, I find myself just staring at her. Also, I guess I'm catching up on some lost looks of the past—looks I was never able to give or receive from her. I know that sounds foolish, but it sounds right to me.

Lying there with her head against white sheets, she now wears a short salt and pepper afro, no longer hair flowing down her back, pressed and pretty, nor an upsweep French roll. No, no more beautiful hair to twirl around her finger.

Suddenly she extended her hand through the rails of her bed reaching for mine. Shaken by this gesture, I paused. Finally I reached out touching the end of her fingers, then grasping her entire hand. I held on, I was pleased. Never having this to happen before between us I didn't know what to do next. She made it easy for me. Her eyes were sad and heart wrenching, a precious moment.

She looked at me and said, "Rheese?"

"Yes, mama."

"Please, please don't give me anymore medicine." Her eyes looked deep, revealing a hollow glare tunneling through, trying to get out.

"Why?" I asked.

"I'm tired. I am so tired and I just don't want to fight anymore."

A sick feeling came and took over my stomach. It was doing acrobatics, flips and flops. I was speechless, but I knew I had to say something and I needed it to come quick.

"You have to take your medicine mama, it's vital to your well being." I said calmly, not knowing if it was for my benefit or hers.

"I don't know about all that wordy crap you're talking about, but if it means keeping me alive, that's why I don't want it anymore." Her breath was shorter and shorter with each word.

"Yes, that's what I mean mama, it's helping to keep you alive."

"Well Rheese let me go. I don't want this kind of life any longer. I'm tired of just laying in this bed. I'm tired of medicine and more medicine, tired of coughing and tired of this thing between my legs that's not a man's penis."

Precious moments interrupted.

"Mama!" I shouted.

"Mama, hell," her voice sounding a little stronger, "I know who I am. What I said is what I meant, so stop with all that got damn mama."

"Okay, have it your way," I was frustrated and annoyed with her way and for the sake of argument I gave in to her request, quickly I changed the subject.

"How about something to eat, how about some eggs?"

"No thanks."

"But you love eggs."

"Today I don't."

"Mama," I pleaded.

"Mama what?" She gave a long pause. "Damn you can say that mama, can't you? Now get your black ass back to our conversation, back to the conversation about the medicine." She wasn't finished with the subject.

"I wish you would continue taking it, taking your medicine mama. You need it."

"I'm tired." She repeated.

"I don't want to hear you talk like that."

"About what, about dying? You've lost your got damn mind, everybody has to die. You got to die! Even if you don't talk about it, you got to do it. Don't make me think you've just been going to church like the other church asses. He made us, He take us, Religion 101."

"I know that." *"Why in the hell was I not in the acceptance of her dying? This is something that I have wanted her to do since I was a child, something I thought would make me happy."* I said to myself.

Then mama interrupted my thoughts with her question, "Well since you know Religion 101 what the hell are you talking about?" "I'm talking about getting to know each other. We've never gotten to know each other."

Trying not to bring up the past or open old wounds, being careful with my words, I refrained a lot. "I'm talking about getting to know my grandmother and all you're talking about is dying."

"It's late Rheese, too late for some things to be put right even, no matter how we want to erase the wrong."

She was taking deeper and deeper breaths as she spoke.

"Whatever you have in mind of me, good or bad, I'll leave you with. I can't change the past. Hate me or love me, no room for in between."

AAGGHH!!! I wanted to scream. It is statements like that that would always piss me off. Cut and dry, she leaves no room to cross over or to make up. Maybe she's afraid I will reject her or say something to hurt her. Keeping me at bay, she makes sure I don't know if I want to hug her or choke her. I got up, turned and walked out of the room without another word said between us.

I began reading my Bible as I sat at the kitchen table, listening to the gospel station on the radio. I sat there for about an hour. I closed my Bible and began preparing myself for another round of aggravation. Sometimes, I think she deliberately says things to raise my blood pressure, because she knows she can get away with it. She knows I'll do anything not to upset her.

She called upon me from her bedroom, "Rheese." I moved swiftly.

"Yes?" as I entered her room.

"Please do me one last favor?"

"I will if I can." still a little annoyed but trying to sound calm.

"You can," she paused, "please don't give me anymore medicine. Tell the nurses I don't want to take anymore, please." She begged desperately.

"Okay." I finally gave in when I heard her cry. I realized she was ready.

"One more thing I need to ask of you Rheese."

"What?"

"Don't forget what else I asked you to do for me. Think about it and you'll remember?"

Without hesitation, "I remember."

"Thank you." She said, she never says thank you, please or I'm sorry. This threw me off balance. I just looked at her. Surprised, not knowing what to think or do. I left the room again and went to the front porch. I sat in the swing and cried.

"Somebody help me!" I wanted to scream. *"I can't handle this!"* She's ready and asking to die. How dare she control me like this again. She controlled me as a child but she has no right to do so now. Leaving me with the decision to tell the nurses what to do whether she will live or die, was just the selfish way of my grandmother.

"How dare she do this to me? God, how I want to hate her but You won't allow it." I wept. After a few minutes and a lot of tears, I declared, "I'll do this

because I've grown tired also, of trying to find a common solution to satisfy us both. I find it hard to see her like this, abrasive or not, she is suffering. The past doesn't seem so important now. I'm empty, I'm confused, this decision is too much but it had to be done. Life has cleared everything out of her, but her last breath.

Remembering a conversation she and I had yesterday.

"I wish I had listened to you Rheese years ago, when you tried to get me to stop smoking. Instead I cursed you out. Now I swapped smoking a pack a day for emphysema. I swapped God's fresh air for a got damned breathing machine. What a damn trade off?"

"I wish you had listened also."

"Since I didn't I guess I'll have to retire early to my dirt nap."

"You need to watch the things you say mama, like cursing or insulting people or hell is where you'll end up."

"I guess I'll see a lot of church asses there. Rheese let me say this if I ain't made my space available for me in Heaven by now, these few bad words won't keep me out. I'm almost ninety and have given up everything in this life, smoking, drinking, shooting and I sho' don't want no sex, so whatever God has for me, I'm ready for it."

"You're right, mama, it's all up to God, it's His decision and not ours to make."

"Rheese?"

"Yes ma'am."

"I should have listened is all I'm saying and I don't want to be given any more medicine is all I'm asking. The damage is done; it can't be reversed and this is no life for me. From the life I used to live, this is no life for me."

"Was she trying to tell me that she was wrong? Was she sorry or was this her way of telling me thank you? Whatever it is she's trying to say, I think I heard it loud and clear."

Saying to myself, "you're welcome mama."

CHAPTER 4

After our brief conversation, mama fell back into a deep sleep. Hopefully, she was feeling much cleaner since I had given her a bath. I sat in the large chair that was in her room and did what I mostly did, crawl into the chair and watch her. I began reminiscing about the stories my grandmother had told me about her past . . .

Mama's life had been a good one, she would always tell me. Proudly saying, "If I die today or tomorrow, the world don't owe me a got damn thing. I can cash in all my chips and won't get a dime back. I lived my life the way I damned well please."

Born April 11, 1916 to Watkin Jackson and Charity Pinkston-Jackson, she was the first of their three girls, then came Mabel and Lucille was the youngest. Always telling me, "Watkin and Charity had all holes and no poles."

Mama was always jealous of her sisters, believing that Lucille was her father's favorite child and Mabel ran a close second. Mama did have some consolation though; she knew Charity loved her dearly. Even though Charity constantly reminded her, 'equally and dearly,' mama only heard dearly. Mama had always called her mother Charity, something her father thought was distasteful and disrespectful. He would become quite angry and upset whenever he heard this, calling it foolishness.

"Charity, she needs to call you 'mama', like the other children."

"It's okay Jack," Charity said.

This would cause his blood to boil, especially hating the fact that his wife pardoned this irritating fault of their daughter.

"Stop supporting her," yelling at the top of his lungs.

Calmly Charity said, "What she calls me does not matter to me; it's only a title. Just as long as she knows her place and respects me as her mother, which she does, I'm happy."

Standing there in his overalls drenched in mud and smelling of the outdoors, he had been working their land which had made them very prosperous. Without cutting it, he grabbed a handful of the chocolate cake Charity had made earlier and began eating. With his mouth full, he began talking. Crumbs flew from his mouth landing in the face of his wife, but not once did she say anything, Charity kept on knitting.

"Since she could talk, Mae never called me nothing but daddy, plus I get the respect," he pointedly said.

"Since she could talk she knew if she didn't say daddy, you would beat it out of her. Then when you get her to do what you wanted, you would ignore her for long periods of time. Is that what you call respect?" Charity pointedly said back.

He raised his hand to slap Charity, but quickly brought his hand down to his side. Licking the icing from his fingers on the other hand, he said, sounding very cross, "I will have won my point."

"But you will have lost a daughter." Charity told him. Expecting to be hit, but the blow never came because this time Charity didn't give him a sense of fear.

Wiping his already dirty, now sticky with icing hands, on his overalls, he said, "I don't want to hear anymore on this subject. I'm through with it so just shut the hell up!" He shouted even louder.

Jack turned to leave the house. Charity prayed that he would leave without incident. He did. Honey had been eavesdropping. When her father left, Honey came into the room where she found Charity knitting and never once looked up at her.

"I heard what daddy said, and if it will keep him from harming you, I'll try to remember or rehearse calling you mama." Honey said to Charity.

"Were you standing somewhere trying to listen?" Charity asked her.

"No ma'am, not trying, but he was so loud."

"Next time, you go outside. You don't need to hear what grown people are discussing. So let me handle your father and you continue calling me what you have grown comfortable with and believe me it will be alright with me."

Loving her mother even more, she said, "Yes ma'am." Pausing for a moment, she asked, "Are you mad with me Charity?"

"Why would you ask me a thing like that?"

"Because you won't look at me."

Looking up from her needle work, she directed her gaze into her daughter's eyes, gestured with her head for Honey to come over, while patting the seat next to her, so Honey would sit down. Honey obeyed. Charity's last request of Honey, as she tapped her jaw with her index finger, was hinting for a kiss. A request Honey was more than happy to fulfill. They continued sitting there.

Charity was knitting and being admired by her daughter without another word said between them. Even when Charity did not speak, she spoke in volumes, her silence was an art she had mastered.

Mama told me that she could watch Charity for hours and she watched her often. The other children had their father, but Mama believed she had much more; she had Charity. Charity never saw a difference in her children. Something Jack rarely did. Over the years he had hammered a wedge between his daughters, causing a division between Honey and her sisters for the rest of their lives.

Watkin Jackson (Jack) was a stern man, no nonsense kind of guy, very striking and handsome. Women would melt in his presence and men cooked their brain with jealousy. Jack was a man of medium stature, straight jet black hair and a very light complexion. His father was white, a man whom he never knew and his mother had features straight from the motherland, Africa. Her hair was nappy and tight, teeth, white and straight and legs long and beautiful. Jack loved his mother but hated the curse of his father. He cared nothing about people constantly telling him of his good looks, which he attributed to his mother; he was all about business.

He would say, "Looks don't put food on the table or pay bills, money does." He was self made. They owned cows, horses, hogs, chickens, turkeys, goats and much land for harvesting his many crops. You name it, Jack probably had it; trees of nuts and fruits, vines of grapes and berries. Their cabinets were filled with preserves and the icebox filled with meats.

Some of his accomplishments came way of selling anything and everything on his regular job he had with the mining company. He would sell his lunch for a price and go hungry for the rest of his shift.

He always believed, he would rather be a hungry man than a broke man, "because if you're not broke you can buy bread for the hunger, but if you're broke, you're still hungry", he would justifiably explain.

A shrewd businessman, if he had a bologna sandwich and sold it, in his other pocket he would have lettuce and tomato to convince them how much more these two items would enhance the taste of the recent purchase of their sandwich. "Sold, to the buyer of the sandwich."

His financial status during the thirties and forties was great and from that time on, his money kept growing. His slogan was, "I'll sell everything but my wife and kids." Some people questioned his morals about the wife and kids, assuming they would be sold if the price was right.

Being of mixed race, Jack never really seemed to belong or fit in with any one race. Whites wouldn't have him and blacks pulled away from him. Why black people thought he was uppity, he didn't know the answer, and as time passed on, he didn't care, but he was bitter. His grandmother was raped by his grandfather, a slave owner, and the same happened to his mother, producing him. When Jack learned the truth, pure hate rose from down deep in the bowel of every fiber of his being. Now that he knew the truth, he wished he had remained in the dark.

He promised himself that his children would not have to go through this curse of skin color and hair texture that had crippled him all his life. There would be no race separation for his children. He made a promise to himself that his wife would be dark as midnight with nappy hair, big nose and even bigger lips. She could be ugly; he didn't care as long as she was human. He shared this information with his mother, who was a mild mannered sweet spirited lady, with an infectious jolly laugh.

"Son ain't cha' a bit yung fur marryin'?" She asked him.

"I don't mean right now, but when I'm ready."

"Dat be put neer all rhat, but ugly makes worsa ugly chil'ren."

"I guess I need to rethink that part, huh?"

"I bleve so, rhat now gwon gits sum schoolin' in yo' head, sum reeding, ritin and rithmatic and yous be jess fine."

She released a laugh heard around the community. Even when things weren't funny, Ozzie found the humor in it. Her laugh was her trademark. Jack couldn't help but to laugh along. They were all each other had. So when Ozzie died a year later, a month before he met Charity, he took it really hard, but he promised his mother that he would finish his schooling and finish is what he did.

As promised, the woman Jack was going to marry, Charity, was of very dark complexion, two shades darker than midnight, medium nose and lips, but most of all she was the most beautiful woman he had ever seen. She had long jet black, kinky hair; her hair and skin almost blended together. With teeth so white, she could lead the way on a moonless night, and she always smelled clean. How he wished his mother had lived to see her. Soon after, Charity and Jack married.

They had everything. Children, money, a home and most of all, they had each other. They didn't just love each other, they liked each other; However, after many years of marriage, something went wrong. Separation and resentment leaked into their harmonious lives. Decay had started to infiltrate his family and home life, and the destruction came rapidly. Jack found it easy to blame Honey and Charity found it easier to stand up for her child, even if it would put her in jeopardy and harms way. The more division and negative feelings grew, the more Honey appreciated Charity.

Learning many things from Charity made Honey very self reliant. She learned how to bake, cook, quilt, sew, mend, clean and even knew how to put just the right amount of Joe Louis whiskey in your coffee. Honey learned to love coffee, morning, noon and night. It was her and Charity's secret and how well Honey could keep their secrets.

Honey loved her mother greatly. Rushing home from school each day, Honey would drop her books anywhere, head straight for her mother to get and give a big hug, before her sisters could make it inside. Honey always had to be first. She always hoped she would find her mother in the kitchen making her famous cornbread that looked and tasted like cake. Lathered in butter just the way she liked it. However, Charity constantly reminded her daughter that she had enough love and cornbread for all her girls.

CHAPTER 5

She was not always a favorite of her sisters, often called 'kiss ass', behind her back. They weren't dumb though, knowing not to ever say such names to her face. She may have been Charity's 'kiss ass' and loving it, but at the same time she would be more glad to give her sisters a good 'kick ass.' Knowing this fact and not wanting anymore bloody noses and fat lips, they stayed smart. This filled Honey with joy and delightful pleasure because she knew she had so much control over them. However, her sisters had a weapon of their own, "Jack". Whenever something went wrong in the house during his absence, he would unleash his anger on Honey, giving her beatings so harsh that they would leave scars, some permanent, on her body.

The very last beating he would execute toward her was the worst. Usually Mabel and Lucille would find fun in her punishment, but not this time, no not this time. Even if they had, Honey would not allow the witches the gratification of her screaming, hollering and rolling around on the floor; she just stood there and took the beating with blood streaming from her arms and legs.

Jack would wear himself thin, before he could break her down. Not wanting to be outdone, he said, "I'm going to leave your crazy ass alone."

Thinking these words would somehow save face and repair his authority, he continued.

"Listen up Charity, if you go in there and baby her, you'll get the same, only worse."

Charity knew he would follow up on every word. She had already experienced his vicious, venomous, violent behavior. Tears formed in the well of her eyes and she felt helpless having only tears for her child. He soon left, or so they thought. Charity quickly rushed over to give comfort to her child only to be surprised by the return of Jack. This made him really upset. Charity had fallen into his premeditated trap.

Jumping up from her seated position on the floor cradling Honey, now with blood stains all over her beautiful floral form fitting dress, Charity moved backwards away from her husband until her legs met the sofa, causing her to take a seat. Grabbing her by the hair, dragging her into their bedroom, he finally got the kicking, screaming and rolling on the floor he desired. The veins protruding from Charity's neck and forehead, made him less of a man.

He began shouting, "How dare you baby that bastard child, how dare you." Over and over he repeated the same thing before he made it to their bedroom and closed the door while Charity pleaded.

"Jack, please stop! Lord, help me. No more please."

She pleaded over and over again. By this time Mabel and Lucille were kneeling behind Honey at the threshold of their parent's bedroom door. Jack had thrown her on the bed and started punching away. She was struck all over her body; he did not care where he landed his blows. Throwing her arms up, she tried to protect her face but her attempts failed. Hearing the terror in her mother's cry, a cry she couldn't take any longer.

Honey turned and went into the kitchen, opened one of the drawers and picked over the knives until she got to the one she chose to use. It was the largest one she could find, short of the size of a meat clever. She walked briskly back toward the bedroom with a blank look on her face, looking hypnotized.

Lucille turned just in time to see her hastily approaching. Meeting her midway of the hall, she said, "Sister", a name they called Honey dearly to her face, "please don't do this," she whispered, "daddy will kill you."

"Well he'd better do me before I do him." She replied.

Mabel turned to find out what the commotion was between them.

"Please." Lucille continued to plead.

"Shut the hell up before I kill you two witches," pointing the blade of the knife in Lucille's direction, then Mabel's.

"Sister you know how daddy is when he's angry, so give me the knife," extending her hand.

"Don't touch me or the knife," Honey snapped.

Her sisters obeyed her command and they didn't touch her or the knife. Remembering once when a dog was charging toward them, they became frightened, except Honey. When the dog leaped for the attack, she gave the dog a right hook, socking the dog between the eyes. The dog was knocked out for at least thirty seconds and when he came around, he ran away. Lucille was amazed the dog lived.

"Sister, don't do this." Mabel cried, "Put the knife down."

Blocking the entrance way, Honey stopped, looked at them both, moving her eyes up and down their scared shaking bodies.

"Whatever you two intend, it's causing you to stand in my way. You better take your got damn intent with you while you move your asses out of my way," Honey replied.

Mabel jumped so fast out of her way that she knocked Lucille to the floor. Proceeding on to the bedroom, Honey gained momentum. One last ditch effort Mabel reached and grabbed the arm holding the knife and held it tight. Honey turned and slapped her so hard her head spun.

Honey stood there for a few moments, then, she said, "You'd better step back or you can get the slap I'm holding in my other hand."

Mabel let Honey handle her business. Now, half of the anger she was holding for her father had to be applied to those two whores.

With tunnel vision and clutching the knife tightly, the only thing on Honey's mind was killing her father. Without another thought, she opened the door, went in swiftly and lunged toward her father, stabbing the back of his right shoulder. She was hoping she had punctured his lung. She struck the same arm that was about to come down on her sweet Charity's beaten and defenseless body. As she pulled the knife out of his body, blood started to ooze out rapidly, staining his blue shirt red. He moaned in agony. While backing away, she held the knife with both hands, continuing to point it at him in attack mode, ready for his next move.

Moaning, he got off Charity and turned around to see what or who had inflicted this great pain. Seeing his daughter holding the knife stained with his blood, he started walking and stumbling over to her. With his arms stretched out and his fingers curved in the strangle position, Honey hurriedly thought, "*Kill or be killed.*"

She was ready for him and whatever he would bring, she would worry about the consequences later.

He yelled out, "I'll kill you, you little ugly bastard!"

She yelled back, "Come on, come on, kill me. I don't care what you do to me anymore; I just don't care, you son of a bitch!" She shouted angrily.

"You can beat me all you want, but I'll be damned if you'll keep on hurting my Charity because you hate me."

"*Your* Charity? What the hell you mean your Charity, what the hell is that all about!?"

He stepped closer as she ignored his questions.

"Keep coming closer so I can ram this knife through your sorry ass body again, come on and let me have the pleasure. This time I hope you will die."

He came closer. She swung the knife; it landed on the left side of his chest traveling across his breast, stopping at the top of his stomach, causing a long gapping wound. The blue shirt was now almost completely red.

"I'll kill you daddy, believe me, I'll kill you."

He stood still. Startled that she was trying to really kill him, he began to move backwards. She realized that he had become defenseless. He came once again toward her. This time it was to leave the room and she allowed him to pass.

Passing Mabel and Lucille, he made his way down the hallway into the kitchen. Holding both hands out in front of him, gesturing to Mabel and Lucille, he said, "look what your sister did to me."

Standing there holding each other and trembling, neither said a word. Honey followed him down the hall with weapon in hand.

Reaching the kitchen, he flopped down hard in the nearest chair, shirt soaked in his blood. The tables had turned on him; now it was his turn to cry out for help. Whimpering like a little puppy and begging the Lord to help him, Jack sounded pitiful but Honey had no pity. Fear still had not yet set in or entered Honey's mind. She was more concerned about Charity's well being and not with the fact that she may be going to jail or a home for juveniles.

She went rushing back to the bedroom to attend to her mother, only to find Lucille and Mabel hovering over her like they were so interested in her safety. With great force, Honey went over and pushed her way through her sisters. Mabel and Lucille tilted like the blow-up rubber man punching bag; only they didn't pop back up so quickly.

Filled with hysterics, once she saw the bloody mess her father had left behind. It broke her heart. Blood was on the pillows, sheets, spread, floor, wall and all over her cut body. Her floral dress was torn to shreds like a Hawaiian grass skirt. Charity's clothes were so raggedy she was almost naked. Tears in Honey's eyes rolled down her face, making her hate him even more. Crawling to the head of the bed, Honey put a pillow in her lap, then placed Charity's head on the pillow.

Honey asked, "Are you alright?"

"I'm alright. I'm fine. It looks worse than it feels."

"We'll get you to the doctor."

Luckily they had a new black doctor in town and the girls knew if they took her to see him, they wouldn't be treated like dirt. Not like they were treated when they needed help in the past and they tried to get decent care from the white doctors in town. They once went into the emergency room of the Hillman hospital, because Jack got a large cut in his hand and he was bleeding quite seriously. The white hospital staff had made them sit and wait and sit and wait.

Sitting and waiting for hours, Jack finally said, "Let's go and let's go now, I've had enough!" He shouted in a strong and loud voice.

This drew no concern from the white medical staff; they glanced at him for a few seconds and looked away, giving their attention back to what they were doing. He was in so much pain and luckily a few weeks prior, the Jacksons had heard of the new black doctor that had come to town. So they sought out to find him and they did. He treated the cut, gave him a tetanus shot, some antibiotics, something for the pain, sutured the cut and told them to leave the bandage and try not to get it wet.

Also, he gave instructions to return in a week so he could check his sutures and change the bandages. Reassuring them that if anything happened, like a fever to come back and see him no matter the time.

Finally the black people in town had someone that cared. The girls knew Dr. Buggs would do the same thing for their mother today, even if Charity didn't have any of Jack's money to pay. He would never allow anyone seeking medical care to suffer or not be treated.

"Please mama, let us take you to the doctor," Lucille said.

Honey rolled her eyes at Lucille as their eyes met, cutting her a razor look. She refrained from saying anything.

"No," Charity responded, trying to release a phony laugh that only made her cringe in pain, grabbing hold of her side to somehow help with the discomfort and agonizing pain. "Charity, you need some medical help," Honey said gently.

"Even if I wanted to go, Jack has control of all our money and we have no money for a doctor bill."

"Dr. Buggs won't care."

"I'll care."

"This is no time for pride."

"I have to have some pride, even when your father is angry, I won't let him take that away from me."

"Who cares about him? I don't. He's not my father. No father of mine would hurt a woman like this. Anyway, this is not about him, this is about you." Honey replied.

Placing her finger over her mouth, Charity hissed, "Shhh! You don't mean that, you're just angry."

"Oh, I mean it."

This time when she hissed, Honey remained silent. Lucille and Mabel also remained quiet.

"I'm proud of my girls and you are all the medicine I need."

"Anyway, let's get you dressed properly and get something to clean your face and body," Lucille said.

This was the only time when either Lucille or Mabel said something and Honey didn't give a bad look or mean gesture toward them.

Lucille jumped up suddenly saying, "I'll go get water, a towel and some soap."

When she brought the warm water, soap and towel, she also brought some antiseptic. Nervously, she whispered, "Daddy is still in the kitchen just sitting there bleeding. Should we do something? Maybe he's dead."

"Good, mission accomplished. I will have kept my promise, and if you don't pay attention and care for our mother, I'll make and keep a promise for you. Mabel, go and see about your daddy," Honey delegated.

"Yes, please go and see about your father," exclaimed Charity with relief.

"Okay."

"That's alright Mabel, I'll go myself," Honey said.

Mabel, Lucille and Charity just looked at each other and said nothing. They didn't know what to say even if they wanted to say something. Fearing if he wasn't dead, she would finish him off.

Easing her way down the hall and reaching the threshold of the kitchen where Jack had slumped down in the chair, she became filled with much disappointment when she heard him groan.

"Damn, he's not dead, ol' low down devil."

She entered into the kitchen, stood at his feet and kicked the bottom of his shoe, causing him to uncross his legs.

"Get up, you asshole, I have no sympathy for you, clean yourself up or go somewhere and get clean, it doesn't matter."

"Help me please," he begged.

"Hell no, why don't you die?"

Struggling, trying to get up from the chair, trembling, he finally stood to his feet. Still not concerned about the consequences she may have to pay and she didn't care, she turned and went back into the bedroom with the others.

"He gone!" Hating to lie to Charity, but this situation was different. She tried to convince herself. Charity loved Honey, but she knew when her daughter was lying and lying was what she was doing.

"Mabel, go and see about your father." Charity told her.

This told Honey in volume that her mother thought she may be lying. She usually trusted what her daughter would say, but this was different.

"Yes, ma'am," said Mabel.

When Mabel got to the kitchen, a wounded Jack was staggering out the back door. When she got back into the bedroom, Mabel announced, "He gone."

Honey thought that Mabel lied because she was afraid to go against her, which suited her just fine.

"See, I told you." Honey said.

"No, you don't understand. He's really gone. He was walking out the back door bleeding."

Everyone figured Honey had lied, Jack was still inside when Honey came back into the room.

"He'll be alright Charity, don't worry he'll be alright." Lovingly she spoke to Charity seeing the concern on her mother's face. Only now Charity's concern was not for Jack, but for her child, praying no one would come to arrest her for possible attempted murder.

No one did.

They all slept in bed together that night. Early the next day around one o'clock in the morning, Charity woke with her left arm aching. She could not move the arm, he hurt her really bad. Then Mabel remembered they had some pain pills left from when their father's hand was cut.

"Wait a minute," she said "there may be something you can take that will help." Mabel figured if it could make their father fall asleep and feel no pain, the wonders it could do for their mother. She ran to the bathroom and was back in a flash, opening her hand to unveil the bottle of pain medicine.

"The label says to take one to two pills every four hours for pain."

Charity was in so much pain that she didn't argue. Mabel began to rub her mother's head and within thirty minutes Charity had dosed off to sleep. Lucille slept through it all.

Honey placed her hand on Mabel and then looked at her as she returned the look and with much surprise, Honey said to her, "Thank you, thank you so much."

"No, thank you Honey, for loving our mother so much, you would die for her, so thank you," Mabel responded.

They gave each other a friendly smile. Then Mabel joined the others and fell asleep.

Years later, mama told me of that night after Mabel told her thank you. She remembered thinking, "*I still don't trust you bitch,*" but she whispered in the ear of a sleeping Charity as she draped her arms around her, "I love you Charity Pinkston Jackson, but as for my father, he's just another chapter closed in my life."

CHAPTER 6

The following day, with the sun starting to peak over the horizon, they quickly gathered some of their things stuffing them in stringed laundry bags. Figuring bags would be much easier than luggage to carry, leaving the rest of the house in tact except for the blood splatter in the room. Although the sun was beginning to rise, it was still dark outside. They hoped to be traveling before any of the neighbors could discover what was taking place.

Honey said, "We shouldn't be worried about the neighbors seeing us, even the early bird is going to miss us."

They all laughed, Charity encouraged them to quiet down and immediately they complied. Shortly thereafter, they found themselves standing at the front steps of Fodie and Callie's house. Fodie was the brother of Charity's father. Fodie was a handsome man, not as good looking as Tipper, her father, but still handsome nonetheless. He was tall with very, toned muscles, brown bag complexion, black hair and very light brown eyes, eyes that changed color, sometimes if you looked at them; they could give you chills. His wife, Aunt Callie was known for her hearty laugh. She was a short wide woman and her face seemed to gain a new mole everyday. Her heart was as big as the moon and her giving gained a new space everyday.

Callie opened the door to their home and there she stood wearing a dress that she made from several flour bags. Her bright smile faded away after she saw the ugly bruises that reached out and told everyone to pay attention and attention Aunt Callie paid.

Swinging her arms, she motioned for them to come in, as she said with sadness in her voice, unlike the usual jubilant manner, "Come on in here you precious thang, come in here and sit down."

They went in as she kept on waving. "My Lawd, you little skinny thangs, let me fix y'all sumtin' ta eat."

They weren't sure if she wanted to feed them because they looked skinny or because they looked pitiful. It didn't matter the problem, Callie always thought a good meal was the solution, and with the aroma coming from the kitchen, they were all inclined to agree. Aunt Callie had to have already been up and out of bed long before their arrival.

"Are y'all hongry?" Callie asked.

"Yes," shouted Honey, "we all are," answering for everyone.

Charity lightly tapped Honey on the hand for this seemingly rude gesture.

Callie saw this action and said, "It's alrhat Charity, I luvs ta eat, as y'all can tell and y'all know I luvs ta cook an' feed folks. So don't fret. Y'all at home an' ain't no shyness 'tween family. Ain't dat rhat chil'ren?" Before anyone could answer she continued, "Now set down an' twiddle yo' fangers or pat yo' feet while I throw sum mo' meat in de fryin' pan."

The aroma of bacon filled the air with its sweetness. Charity, Lucille, Mabel and Honey were sitting at the table discussing what flavor the bacon was. One said it was hickory, one said maple and the last guess was ham.

However, Honey said "handcuffs." Everyone laughed. Charity gripped her side in pain when she tried to laugh. Callie heard their conversation, especially about the handcuffs, but she kept on cooking. Figuring they would talk when they were ready.

Screaming at the top of her lungs, she called her husband for breakfast and to surprise him with their company.

"Fodie!" No answer.

"Fodie! Git down here an' get yo' breakfast now 'fo it get cold! Y'all needs ta grab one of dem dere plates and tiny pitch fawks ova dere an' come help yo'self ta sum good eatin'. I got bacon, ham, sausage, grits, gravy, biscuits, eggs an' fried 'taters. Eat all y'all want 'cause I cooked plenty. Fodie! Brang it on down here, yo' eggs gettin' cold." Callie yelled again.

His voice came from near by. "I heard ya woman, I's comin as fast as I can git dere."

Turning the corner to come into the kitchen at the threshold, he stopped in his tracks. He was set on pause, his eyes stretched wide and mouth fell open when he saw them sitting at the table eating breakfast.

"What da hell . . . ?" He said.

Coming over to the table, Charity stood up to receive a hug from him, holding his arms open wide. He hugged her, she winced. With excitement of seeing her, he moaned, "Ummm, what a sho' 'nuff surprise, makin me feel betta dan a hot butta biscuit."

He pushed Charity away from him, but held onto her shoulders with both hands. He took a moment to look at her, but never once did he ask about the bruises. Finally letting Charity go, he motioned for the girls to get up and give him a hug.

After the reunion, Fodie grabbed himself a plate and piled the food high, eating all he put on his plate. He didn't believe in wasting food. He remembered as a child many nights having to go to bed hungry.

They never saw Aunt Callie eat anything; she was always busy cooking, pouring coffee, washing dishes and holding conversations, telling stories of her childhood. Anyway, they could tell she wasn't suffering from lack of nourishment.

All morning long they laughed.

After breakfast Aunt Callie asked, "Alrhat now, does anybody want anythang else, sum coffee, juice, milk?".

Some said no, others nodded yes.

After filling each request, she began cooking and cleaning her large kitchen, "Oh well den I guess I's put my dinner on."

"Dinner?" Honey said to herself. *"Cooking one meal after another, does she ever leave the kitchen? Maybe that's why they don't have any children? She must be doing her best work in the wrong room."*

"I'll help." Charity said.

Taking a seat at the table and no longer being able to hold her peace, Callie pulled her chair close to where Charity sat. By this time no one was left in the kitchen but Honey, Charity and Callie. Lucille and Mabel had followed Fodie outside. Aunt Callie reached out and placed her hand on top of Charity's.

"Let me say dis ta ya chile," Aunt Callie stated, "If ya find yo'self sumwhere, anywhere and needs me, don't ya hesitate ta call on me, 'cause if ya do, consider me dere already."

Charity responded, "I will."

"I means it. I may has married inta dis family, but I's true family an' I luvs my family." Callie said.

"I know you do, I just don't want to bother anyone with my problems," Charity began.

Slapping her hand down on the table and pointing her finger in the direction of Charity, her voice barely above a whisper, Callie said, "Don't ya ev'a in yo' life nor mine, let me hear ya talk 'bout 'xcluding yo' family when ya need 'em; next time I won't be slapping dis table. Dat's what family is fo', ta help anyway dey can, ya' understand me?"

"Yes, I do." Charity responded.

They began to cry, even Honey. Callie got up from her chair and went over and gave Charity a hug. "Evr'ythang gon' be alrhat, ya bes b'leve, 'specially when I finish tellin' God all 'bout it."

"Amen!" Honey shouted, "Amen!"

Charity and Callie chuckled.

"Alrhat now everybody," Callie said very loudly, "I has me an appointment wit sum food in dis kitchen an I promised it dat I would cook it." Her signature laugh escaped her mouth causing a chain reaction.

Honey and Charity didn't think what she said was funny. They were laughing at the infectious sounds that Callie made. Charity was trying hard to stop laughing because this produced more pain to her side. When Honey saw the discomfort on her face, she got up so fast, she drew concern to Callie, but she was back so fast that she didn't have time to wonder what was going on. Honey gave Charity two pills and a glass of water. She swallowed the pills and looked over at Callie, then told her what happened the night before.

Shock and disbelief flooded Callie's thoughts. Then anger took over as she stated, "Maybe I don't need ta go ta God wit dis, I needs ta go wit Smif and Wesson."

Honey snickered.

"I hate y'all had ta go through dat, but you's safe now." Aunt Callie said. Changing the subject, "We's be having fo' supper, collard greens wit ham hocks, fried corn, macaroni and cheese, potato salad, black eyed peas, catfish, yams, cornbread and my famous apple pie. We's gon' celebrate like Christmas. 'Cause we's need ta be in de mood fo' gift givin', a butt kickin' to Jack." This time Charity laughed.

Honey would have wondered what army was going to eat all of that food, but after seeing the mound that Uncle Fodie had devoured at breakfast this morning, her thoughts subsided.

"Everythang we's gon' be eatin is by way of Watkins Jackson." Realizing what she said, she covered here mouth. Seconds later she continued. "Don't mean ta keep callin' dat name."

"It's okay," said Charity, "I'm not offended."

Getting up from the table and clapping her hands together and making a little skip, Aunt Callie said, "I's sho' glads ta hear dat, 'cause I don't want ta cook no upset food. Whatsinever we's gon' eat fo' supper is free food from dat good fo' nuttin' Jack an' we's want it ta stay free as long as us can gits it."

Honey was surprised that the food was freely given by her father, stating, "I can't believe daddy gave you anything free with his tight ass."

"Watch your mouth little lady." Charity rebuked her daughter as she started to feel the effects of the pain medicine.

"It must have been some anger I've held hostage since yesterday," Honey responded.

"Dat son-of-a-bitch would have mo' dan two holes in his ass," Aunt Callie ranted.

They began to laugh, not only at whatever she would say, but at all of her body gestures. She was funny.

"And ta answer yo question, yes ma'am I didn't pay a red cent for us ta have dis here feast, an' we enjoyin' it in our mind already," Aunt Callie said.

Kicking her leg up in the air, Aunt Callie created a song to sing. "♫ We has food ta eat, Thank God fo' our meat, we so proud ya knows we evun has sum ta go.♫ The tune sounded like God Bless America, she sounded horrible, but again she was funny, Honey thought to herself.

She did a jig across the floor, then she stopped in the middle of her dance and saw Charity and Honey enjoying every minute.

"Let me stop 'fo I blow a fuse. Sumhow dis kitchen make me act giddy an silly, but dis is a happy place, my stompin ground. A place where, not only Pops and me have our meals, but it's a place where we solve a lot of our problems. De rest of our problems are solved upstairs, if ya know what I mean."

"No Aunt Callie, I don't know what you mean, tell me," Honey said.

"Okay," she paused, "rhat after da milk dries from behind yo ears. Now let me start my supper; y'all git out an' git sum rest."

They took her up on that and went upstairs and went to bed.

It was late when Honey and Charity woke up only to find Lucille and Mabel had fallen asleep also. Charity woke the girls so they could eat. When they got to the kitchen, Aunt Callie and Uncle Fodie were seated at the table across from one another holding hands.

Clearing her throat, "Are we interrupting something?" Charity asked.

Uncle Fodie released her hands and stood up. His overalls were dirty and so were his hands and one of the hook closures was undone and flipped onto his back.

"No, no, y'all fine. We jus thanking God fo' our blessing. Thanking Him fo' y'all and y'all bein safe."

He then got up washed his hands and went over to the cupboard to get some plates for them to eat dinner. He took for granted that they were hungry and he would be right on the money.

"I want to thank you and Callie to allow us to live here and treat us like royalty. Never once did we feel the need to hurry out of here, nor were we treated with a cold shoulder. You left us with our dignity. Instead of asking us to leave, you've extended an invitation to stay as long as we need." Charity said.

"Hell, y'all can move in; it's ain't lac' we don't have 'nuff room in dis big ass house. Oh, excuse my French, but y'all know what I mean an y'all can put dat in yo' pipe an' smoke it." Uncle Fodie said.

"Yes we do and ya'll can take us up on dat." Aunt Callie added.

"We'll keep that in mind." Charity said.

After devouring his meal, getting up from the table where everyone was eating, Uncle Fodie said, "Now ladies, do whatsineva y'all does best, draw on new faces, plot ta spend my money. Now I gots ta go keep money comin' so y'all got money ta spend."

Throwing her dish towel at him, Aunt Callie said, "Get yo'self outta here tellin' dat 'spensive lie an' if ya got all dat money an' been hidin' it dis long, you in fo' it buddy."

Everyone laughed, especially Honey. She said, "There is so much laughter, I could live here forever."

Before leaving the kitchen, Fodie said one more thing, "On a serious note, lil' lady, at dis house, fo'ever starts today."

"Chile my husband speaking gospel and I agree."

Tears started rolling down Charity's face. "I'm sorry I didn't mean to mess up everything by crying but I can't help it, you two have always been so good to me."

"Chile, de only thang dat gets messed up 'round here is Fodie's old overalls, ya see when family luvs an' starts ta git a wrinkle 'round here, we set at dis table an talk till we press it out. Our conversations means sumthin' our luv is true," Aunt Callie said.

Without warning a voice barreled into the conversation. "At our house, we would need a mighty big iron," Mabel complained.

"At dis house we start out wit two big irons 'til we don't need nuttin' but dis big ole oak table an' since we done found dis big piece of wood, we's done a lot of pressin an now mos' all our wrinkles be flat. So don't y'all eva give up. Give out but don't give up," Aunt Callie explained.

"Aunt Callie, you sure are an inspiration. God knew what He was doing when He put you in our lives," Charity said complimenting her.

"I's don't know 'bouts inspiration but I's know God ain't never wrong. Now," slapping her hands down on her knees, "if y'all ladies don' finished eatin', I's gonna git dese dishes washed."

"Let me help," Charity said.

"Nope. Y'all jest sit back an' relax an' git ready fo' bed; I'ma take care of dis. 'Sides, if y'all stay fo'eva, b'leve me dis will change an' den y'all can catch up on washin dishes. Agreed?"

"Agreed," Charity said.

They all went off to bed except Honey. "I'm going to keep Aunt Callie company a little while longer."

Charity kissed Honey on the forehead then followed the girls upstairs.

Honey waited until she was sure that the coast was completely clear. "Aunt Callie?"

"Yes chile."

"I want to talk to you."

"I kinda figured dat out when ya stuck 'round 'cause I know ya ain't stayin' ta look at my backside."

"First, I'm sorry we didn't visit more, living so close and all."

"Honey, yo' 'pologies ain't got no merit here, 'cause it ain't necessary. Now what's on yo mind chile?" Aunt Callie asked.

"I've heard that my daddy is going around telling everyone that he was in a street fight and sent us to stay with you because him being hurt, he couldn't protect us if trouble came to the house. He's lying," Honey explained.

"Let it go chile, let it go," Aunt Callie said.

"I want people to know that his own daughter beat the hell out of him."

"Dat's jus too much anger fo' dat small body. Listen ta me, if ya neva lis'en ta me no mo'. Dere's time ta keep thangs an' a time fo' lettin' 'em go. So let go chile, let it go." Aunt Callie told her.

"You've already said that," her voice rising with frustration. Knowing her frustration, Callie allowed her (Honey's) tone to roll off her, like the old saying goes, like water on a duck's back, allowing her to release the tension brewing inside.

"It's unfair I need to hold on to this! I don't want to let go. He hurt me and what's more he hurt Charity; she didn't deserve that. I hate him!"

"Baby," she said while pulling up a chair next to Honey. "Hate is a dangerous thang ta carry 'round. It can be so heavy it will bust, infectin' yo' life fo'ever. One day chile you'd be lookin' 'round an life be passed on by an you be don' missed out on a heap of thangs 'cause ya let hate eat yo' insides up."

"I hate him," she continued to cry.

"Take my advice chile an' do yo'self and all de ones ya love a favor an' let it go. Hatin' yo' father while yo' mama loves him can only brang heartache."

"It won't be my heartache."

"Ya may thank de heartache ain't yo's. De heartache may not be yo's, but don't leave de possibility out. Anyhow's, you's can bet yo' bottom dollar yo' mama will be caught smack dab in de middle."

"I can't do this thing you're asking me to do, at the snap of a finger."

"You can do whatsinever you set yo' mind on."

"No, I can't."

"If ya keep tellin yo'self ya can't, then ya can't."

"I can only try to forgive that son of a bitch."

"Hey! Watch yo' mouth. Ya been 'round yo' uncle too long."

"I'm sorry."

"What if I don't fo'give yo' sorry . . . ?"

Hesitance came before she would answer. Then she smiled, "Alright I get it."

"I promise ya feel betta."

"I really feel better knowing that son of . . ."

"Dat mouth young lady," interrupting Honey in mid sentence.

"I can't help it when I'm talking about my daddy."

"Well I won't help it if I can't keep dis fis' out yo' mouf if you cuss again." Holding her fist up, she continued, "So ya stop talkin' 'bout him an' ya go to bed an' get sum rest; dat way I won't bruise my knuckles an' ya git ta keep yo' teeth."

"What about you, getting rest, Aunt Callie?"

"I don't need much res', but I's be up when I'm finished, but I's can't finish wit ya stayin down here."

Honey gave Callie a kiss on the cheek and said, "Good night, see you tomorrow."

"Dat's a sure bet an' good night ta ya too."

CHAPTER 7

Having been housed with Callie and Fodie for a while, Charity had begun to feel guilty since she had no money to contribute to any of her aunt and uncle's household expenses. Getting up a little bit earlier, she had hoped she could prepare some coffee before everyone else got up for the day and have a private talk with Callie and Fodie.

She dashed into the bathroom, brushed her teeth, washed all of her important parts and slipped into one of her comfortable house dresses. She dashed down the steps, only to hear voices coming from the kitchen and the aroma of coffee brewing. She walked in and greeted them with a warm, "good morning," and a kiss on the cheek of each.

"Mo'nin," Callie and Fodie, said in harmony.

"There's just no surprising you Aunt Callie."

"What'cha mean honey?"

"I had plans of getting downstairs early enough to get coffee started and maybe some biscuits in the oven, but I just can't seem to get down here before you."

"Yo' Uncle Fodie beat ya gettin down here."

They laughed their signature laughs, loudly, laughs that could wake up the dead.

Gathering her composure, Callie said, "Baby, ya did surprise ole Aunt Callie."

"How?"

"When ya wuz up, dressed, down here an' ready ta cook an' dat clock only reads five fifteen (5:15) an' dat be a.m. So yeah, I be surprised an' pleased."

Callie could see the disappointment and seriousness on Charity's face and so could her uncle.

"Well, I'm glad I please you. But can I ask another question?"

"Ya don't has ta ax po'mission ta ax questions 'round here, all ya gots ta do is ax. So go 'head chile ax yo' question."

"Tell me what time do you get up or do you go to bed? You don't have to answer Uncle Fodie because you are not consistent."

He jerked his head slightly and tilted it to the side and said to Callie, "And don't ya laugh woman." She only smiled.

"I go's ta bed late, but I wakes up early an' start my day an' I pulls de covers up ova dat ol' rooster shoulders so he can turn ova an' sleep a lil bit longer 'fo his shift ta crow an' wake er'body up."

Charity couldn't help but to laugh out loud. Soon, they were all laughing, until Fodie stopped laughing and interrupted their fun.

"It show is good, Charity, ta see ya laugh."

"You know unc', it feels good to laugh, inside and out."

Callie reached over and put her short fat hand on top of her and gave her a wink.

"There's something else that I would like to talk to you about, Aunt Callie and Uncle Fodie, if this time is a good time."

"Time 'round here always be good," said Fodie, "'memba ya home."

Giving her encouragement, Callie had to say something, because she could feel Charity's hands start to perspire.

"Good or bad, say it, we's tough."

Pulling her hand from underneath her aunt's she stood up from the chair and walked behind it and grabbed hold tightly.

Nervous, she held even tighter onto the chair. Charity had begun her own guilt brigade; especially since she had no money to contribute to any of the household needs.

"We have been here almost a month and we don't want to wear out our welcome. Even when it's relatives, they can become a strain emotionally and mental."

Fodie jumped up from the chair, sounding angry.

"Too late yo' welcome already wo' out."

Charity's mouth flew open; her heart raced and her grip became tighter. So tight, she must have been wringing out her hand, as a stream of sweat rolled down the chair.

He leaned back, cupping his balled fist to cover his mouth, like he was singing into a microphone, and then released a yelp. Finally he said, "Lis'en here lil lady, lac' I said when ya furst got here, stay long as ya lac', ya home. Now dat's de end of dat, okay. De only way ya pay me money, it gots ta be a million dolla bill, not, ten, twenties and hundreds; dat's too much paper. It gots to be one bill an' only one bill, a million dolla bill. If ya don't have dat, we ain't got nuttin' ta have convite 'bout no mo', okay. 'sides yo' husband feed us well."

"Okay, but what's a convite?"

"When some knuckle head gots ta have convasation an' invite ya ta come in and dey ain't sayin' nuttin' yo' ears wants ta hear."

This made her feel better. She took in a deep breath, exhaled and said with a smile, "thank you, thank you, thank you, until the end of time thank you."

"Now dat we has dis straight, let us hear what my wife been cookin' dis mo'nin 'cause it sho' mo' smell good an' I's know it's gon' taste good."

Meanwhile, When Jack learned his family had left, he was crushed. Sorrowful, he vowed and became determined to win his family back to him and home. It took him two days to find where they were and almost four weeks to heal enough to go and visit his family. He notified Callie and Fodie concerning his desire and wanted them to allow him to visit his family in their home. They agreed, only after they received the go ahead from his wife.

They gave him the green light. Honey had once again been eavesdropping on their conversation; she became belligerent. She came into the kitchen, still in her gown, her night cap must have come off her head as she slept because her hair was wild, all over her head and she was barefoot. She began shouting, "Why Charity, why?"

"He said that he was very shame of how he treated us and that he was very sorry and it will never happen again." Charity tried to exclaim to her daughter.

"Damn right, he's sorry, a damn sorry ass."

Offended by her words, but Charity knew this was the wrong time to reprimand her. She was still hurting and had not healed on the inside.

But, Uncle Fodie didn't care about the healing, so when Charity wouldn't reprimand her, he told Honey Mae in a very firm voice, "Watch yo' mouth lil gurl, dis yo' mother and she is jus' as old over you as de day you wuz bo'n. So roll out yo' red carpet of respect ta say what'cha needs ta say."

"I'm sorry Charity and you deserve respect, but you also deserve someone better?"

"Listen baby . . ." Charity started.

Interrupting her mother's next words, "No! You listen. If you think for one second that I will trust my face and body not to be abused by that son of a bitch you call a husband, you can give it more thinking. If it means losing you or you beating me down because I said a bad word, then SO BE IT!"

With tears running everywhere, the thought of not being with her mother was unbearable.

Charity pulled her child's face into her bosom and they both cried. Holding her daughter by the shoulders, she gently pushed her to arms length, so she could look into her face, then she said, "I've already asked Uncle Fodie and Aunt Callie, if you could remain living with them for a while and they said yes."

This did bring some consolation to Honey's aching heart and disturbed mind. "If you're going to stay with daddy, it will be a long while."

"Sweetheart, I wish you would change your mind."

"And I wish you would change yours. Just think Charity, if I went back with you to live, I would eventually kill him or vice versa. In my sleep I would be killing him. I do that now. So no, I can't live with him in a house ever again."

"I love you Honey Mae," Charity exclaimed.

"No, you love him," Honey said.

Taking a very long stare into her mother's teary eyes and cold as ice, she turned, walked away and out of the house; never once did she look back. Hurting and now drowning in her own tears, she said, "I love you Charity, but goodbye to another chapter in my life."

Having not spoken to her beloved Charity for the last two days, Honey realized the day had come for Jack to come for his family, all except Honey Mae. This crushed Honey Mae, but she was too obstinate to ever give in, whether there was a change in her father or losing her Charity. She didn't give a damn about her sisters, even though, for the last two months the girls had gotten along and gathered a relationship, or so Lucille and Mabel thought.

Things began to unravel after Honey's last talk with their mother. They knew there had been a change, but neither knew why. Saddened by the fact, she would be left behind, they went onto the back porch where Honey was standing, smoking a cigarette, a habit she had found to be very satisfying.

Surprised, Mabel rushed over to her. "Honey, are you crazy? Don't you know the trouble you'll be in if you are caught with a cigarette?"

"Since I didn't get any jail time for attempted murder, how much time do you think they'll give me for this cigarette?"

Lucille, finding the logic quite agreeable said, "that's true, so let me take a puff."

After a moment, between the three of them the cigarette was almost finished. While the sound of laughing and giggling floated into the open back door, Callie emerged from inside. Mabel scrambled to stomp out the still lit butt of their shared piece puff.

"Y'all don't gots ta hurt yo'self tryin' ta hide thangs from me. I has ESP and 'sides I can smell an' see da smoke floatin' in da air."

They giggled even more. Callie had the knack for making the girls feel comfortable in her presence and she was trustworthy.

"Gurls, y'all daddy is ready ta take y'all home," Callie said.

Honey's attitude went from laughter to anger. "So!"

"Hey! Hol' yo' ho'ses. I's not da enemy so watch yo' mouth," Callie said.

"I'm sorry." Then without another word, Honey turned and ran off.

Lucille was about to run after her, but Callie grabbed her by the arm and said, "Naw, she be jus fine. Let hur be. Leave hur wit' hur thoughts."

Guiding the girls into the house, Lucille and Mabel went to greet their father. Not quite sure how they really felt but they were glad to see him. Jack was on time, three o'clock p.m. was the time he had promised he would arrive, not one minute before or after. He was there, three o'clock sharp.

Fodie opened the door and greeted Jack with a strong welcome as Charity stood in the background, peeping around the corner, watching as he interacted with Fodie.

"Hey man." Jack said.

Extending his hand, they shook. Then Fodie used is other hand to pull Jack across the threshold.

"Come on in here an' sit yo'self down. Can we git you sum'in?" Fodie asked.

"Yes, my family," Jack responded.

"Coming rhat up. Calling de Jackson family," Fodie shouted, "Y'all gots a daddy an' a husband at da doe'," Fodie said.

Emerging from her hiding spot, Charity came from around the corner. Their eyes locked for the first time since that dreadful night. Approaching each other slowly, they came together, hugged and gave a passionate kiss. They released each other when Mabel and Lucille came tumbling through the entrance.

Immediately, he did notice that Honey Mae was not with them. No matter how excited Mabel and Lucille were, he was disappointed that Honey wasn't there. For the first time he was genuinely hurt and was really hoping that the two of them could heal old wounds. If not now, hopefully one day they would heal, mentally and emotionally.

However Fodie and Callie were overjoyed by the thought of having Honey in their home and lives, even if it's only on a day-to-day basis. Day to day turned into a year and a year turned into two. Their lives revolved around Honey Mae; she was the center of their world. Giving her all the love they could and with no reservation she gave back.

It didn't matter the amount of love, Honey Mae missed Charity. They had not seen each other for two years. Charity tried, but Honey Mae refused. Thinking, with Charity came Jack and she was not ready to forgive him or ever would she.

Always aware of Honey's feelings, Fodie, a few days later, called for a family conference. They gathered at the great kitchen table where most of their brilliant decisions were made, or so they said.

"Honey pot," Fodie's new name for her, "yo' ole uncle needs ta ax ya a very impo'tant question."

"Okay." She responded.

"Is ya sick an' ti'ed of us an' ready ta go home?"

Shaken by his unwarranted question and not knowing it's source or origin, she answered abrasively before thinking.

"Hell no! I'm sorry uncle, but that question really caught me off guard."

"Cussing lac' dat, ya mus be ready ta go home. Git hur bags Callie, so she can pack 'em."

Callie didn't say a word, nor did she move. She was confused and thought her husband had lost his mind.

Looking into her uncle's eyes, she said, "You're joking with me right?"

"Well, I mighta been, 'til ya cussed me out."

"No, I didn't. I've used stronger words than that when I'm upset and you never wanted to send me away."

"I can say, I has heard ya cuss sum of yo' friends when ya thank grown folks ain't lis'enin' an' learnin' me an' Callie sum new cuss words."

"I did?" Honey asked, acting quite innocent. "I'm really sorry."

"No, you ain't."

"Honest, I'm telling the truth."

Not knowing whether her husband was playing or speaking in truth, Callie rose from her chair, taking her damp dish towel and slapping her husband across his shoulders several times as he tried to dodge each blow, but was unsuccessful in his attempts.

"I don't know what ya be doin', but ya don' piss me off wit yo' mess," Callie said.

"I wuz jus havin me sum fun," Fodie said, still dodging the feverishly swinging towel.

"You don' took yo' jokes too far!" she yelled. "And b'leve me I ain't playing." Making her way around to where Honey Mae was sitting, gripping the child by the back of her head, leading her face into her large bosom, Callie hugged her.

"Chile, don't pay him no mind."

"I'm okay. I know how Uncle Fodie can tease," Honey nervously said.

Releasing her grip Callie said, "Good."

Fodie was across the room, laughing his ridiculous laugh. "I sho nuff sorry ladies, fo'give me." Walking toward them slowly and receiving acceptance for his apology, he hugged them both, but he still had things he wanted to say to his niece.

"Honey pot, I called ya fo' one reason an' one reason only. Are ya . . ." Before he could say another word, Honey answered, "I'm happy, I don't want to go home, I am home."

"You don' answered my questions. We wants ya ta be happy here an' ta know dat we love you."

"I know."

Aunt Callie crying and sobbing said, "We wants ya ta know dat we do love ya, but we's neva gon' stand in yo' way to live wit Charity and Jack."

"If Charity has left daddy or he has died, come to me about having a kitchen table discussion or about me going back, but for right now, he's a closed chapter in my life," Honey told them pointedly.

CHAPTER 8

School season was about to begin and morning had come too soon for the teenager. Callie had to call her several times; the last time was a threat before Honey Mae gathered herself to move from under her covers. Sitting on the side of her bed, Honey's eyes were closed when the knock on her bedroom door frightened her. She stood straight up and now her eyes were wide open. "I'm up."

"Jus' checkin." Callie yelled through the door. "Breakfus ready. So hurr'up 'fo it get cold, an' don't make me come back up here."

"Okay, I'll be right down," Honey Mae answered.

She could hear the heavy sound of her aunt's footsteps as she left from her door, making her way back downstairs smiling and shaking her head. Twenty minutes later, young lady emerged, dressed in a pale yellow shirt with white polka dots, a pale yellow skirt, both pieces starched so heavy, they could stand on their own and if dropped they would probably shatter. White bobbie socks and sneakers, she looked lovely. Callie turned away from the stove to have a look and she couldn't help but give Honey Mae high compliments.

"Chile is ya goin' ta school or ta da prom? If I could whistle, I would. De teachers need ta brang ya da apple. Now sit yo'self down an' have sum viddles." Callie always cooked for an army of people—bacon, eggs grits, potatoes and her famous homemade buttermilk biscuits.

Suddenly the back door swung open and Fodie entered full of energy. "How's my gurl dis morning?" He asked.

Callie and Honey Mae both answered harmoniously at the same time. "I'm good."

He laughed and they joined in. Soon Honey Mae was on her way to school.

"See you this evening," she said as she waved goodbye.

"See ya." Callie called out to her. "If ya don't learn nuttin else know dis, all dat ya can add up today plus sum will neva equal ta how much us luv you."

Fodie whispered to Callie, "I couldn't say dat no betta."

She playfully slapped his shoulder and went about her duties in the kitchen while shaking her head.

"We have dat child spoil rotten an' I love it," Fodie said.

Honey Mae walked alone toward the small, white, chipped paint, wood framed school. It was only able to house a few students and it needed some overdue repairs. She caught a glimpse of her sisters quite a distance ahead causing her to slow down her pace to a stroll.

Coming up behind her, horses could be heard, their hooves clopping down the rocky dirt road as they approached rapidly. The sound had its own beat, causing Honey Mae to slightly bounce with her walk. The musical sound drew closer and closer until the sound was close enough that she could smell the horse's breath. Without looking around, from the corner of her eye she could see the tip of the horse's nostrils.

Frightened by this new experience, she screamed, almost falling into the ditch that traveled alongside the side of the road; somehow she regained her balance. Not being very fond of animals, especially very large ones, she became overly anxious. Trying to gain her composure, she wanted the driver to hear and understand the sound of her firm voice.

Clenching her teeth she said, "Are you out of your got damn stupid ass mind?"

Just like that, she had forgotten to control her foul mouth, as she brushed the dust from her fresh clothes, the dust that his wagon wheels had created.

"Sorry ma'am didn't mean to scare you," came the deep voice from the driver of the wagon.

"Sorry my ass, asshole," she hissed.

She finally looked up to see the face of the person that was responsible for causing this fiasco. He was the best looking, dirty man she had ever laid eyes on. He was wearing overalls, no shirt and one of the hooks was undone, giving view of his large biceps. She could see each ripple of his chest, not having one ounce of fat. She wanted to refrain from the harsh tone and ugly words she had hurled at the apologetic man, but she felt it was too late and she refused to eat humble pie. So she continued to be tough and unladylike.

"Idiot," she said.

"I'll be anything you would have me to be ma'am, and I'm sorry for getting you dirty," he apologized, even though he saw not a speck of dirt or dust on her.

"Well you need to be more careful," Honey Mae said.

"I'll take that under advisement and I'll have your clothes cleaned, looking good as new. I must say this, even if it gets me in deeper trouble," he said with a pause, "I lost my focus when those hips of yours was waving at me like a pair of hands and your skirt popped with each step you took."

She couldn't help but smile at his humor, but she tried not to let him see her facial expression. She began walking away as though she wasn't interested and wanted to end their conversation. Quite the opposite, she wanted to hang onto this good looking mass of a man's attention as long as she possibly could; forever would be long enough. *Coy.*

"I need to go before I'm late for school," she said to him.

"Little lady, if I may be so bold, I'll give you a ride so you won't be too late and my horse won't be worn out trying to keep up with you," he stated.

Again, before thinking, she blurted out, "Not in that damn thing. Besides I don't know you and I don't climb up in no strange men's trash wagon. I won't even climb up in a trash wagon with someone I know."

With her head held high, looking straight ahead, she picked up speed and momentum.

"If you hold your head any higher, something is going to fly up your nose and if you walk any faster you'll burn the sole off those pretty shoes, leaving a path of leather," he said to her.

She found his humor something she could get use to, but she couldn't allow him to see how much she was enjoying their talk and time together. She was feeling comfortable with him and didn't even know him.

"Slow down little sweet lady so I can talk to you." "Like I said, I have to get to school and I don't want to be late on my first day."

Although she was lying, she could care less about going to school, first day or last day. If it wasn't for Callie and Fodie, she would have given the whole school concept a swift kick in the behind. Hurting them was the last thing she would ever want to do. Besides, if she didn't show up, the two bitch informants, Lucille and Mabel, would set off the alarm and she didn't feel like kicking ass.

"I won't make you late sweet lady, I'll eat my horse if I do." He replied.

"You're lying, I don't believe you." She said to him smugly.

"Don't believe which, being late or eating my horse?" he asked.

"It doesn't matter," she responded.

"That's where you're wrong, everything about you matters," he said slyly.

She thought that was a wonderful thing to say. She would love to talk to him the rest of the day, but she started a slow trot trying to make him believe she wasn't interested. She soon turned off the road onto the property of the school.

He called out to her, "Hey."

She didn't turn around.

"What's your name?" He said.

Quickly Honey started to run until she arrived at the school house steps then vanished behind the school doors. She thought of him the rest of the day.

The following morning Callie didn't need to call but one time and Honey Mae was up and almost dressed. Rushing downstairs, not wanting breakfast, Honey Mae kissed Fodie and Callie and like a freight train, she zipped right out the door past them.

"What da hell was dat?" Fodie asked his wife.

Callie paused for a few seconds, put down her coffee cup, looked at her husband with a big smile and said, "Sum folk call it, luv."

Leaving home early and walking slowly, Honey Mae was hoping to see that fine, good-looking stranger again. She was already planning to have his last name and didn't even know his first or if he was already married.

Finally, she heard the pounding of horse shoes against the stony path, making her feel a feeling she had never experienced before, except with her mother, but yet the feeling was different. It was a feeling of, you're invited to come inside of me, take your shoes off and get comfortable. She silently gave him permission to enter into her private world.

The sound came up rapidly behind her, then . . . there was the voice, deep and commanding acknowledgement. The hooves quieted into a lull until they stopped.

"Good morning sweet philly," he said.

Turning her face to look at him, she tried to get as much mental picture her brain could hold. Soon she knew that she had enough eye wear until tomorrow. She turned away, very sassy, "Isn't a philly a damn horse?"

He deliberately said things to get her fiery energy started. Only knowing her for one day, he knew her.

"They're beautiful and wild," he said.

"They're still a damn horse."

"Being so pretty, how did you get such a foul mouth?"

"Yes, I've been told. I learned from the best, my father." She told him, sounding proud of this fact.

"After people told you, you didn't try to do anything about it?" he asked.

In her way of thinking, she took that statement as a personal insult, which unleashed her uncontrollable anger. "I do whatever the hell I want and keep your nosey ass the hell out of my business." She said waving her hand and shaking her finger.

He had to think quickly so he didn't lose before he got a chance to win.

He said to her, "I like foul-mouthed, hand waving, finger twisting, no nosy ass taking, stay the hell out of your business, pretty, bow-legged, big butt, skirt-popping, shapely kind of women." Then he took in a deep breath and released a loud exhale. "Wooooooah!"

No longer could she hold it; she burst into laughter. Shocked by his response, she said, "You have a dirty mouth, what are you going to do about it?"

"I like that." He said pointing in her direction.

She was still so broken up with laughter she could hardly say anything else. She thought to herself, "*I'm going fishing. This man will be my husband. I like how he makes me laugh.*"

"While I have you attention and know you like my humor, I'm charging for my performance. So before you go into school, do me a favor, please," he stated.

Still chuckling, but with better composure she asked, "What?"

"Will you tell me your name so if I die before I see you again and go to heaven, I'll have something sweet sounding coming from my lips?"

"You're not going to die," she said while thinking again to herself, "*at least not before I have your babies.*" "Honey Mae, Honey Mae Jackson."

"A sweet name for a strong sweet lady. Well Ms. Jackson, you sure are beautiful, if you don't mind me saying this?"

Honey Mae was holding her books high in front of her mouth, swinging her body slightly from side to side, acting girly. The same way she hated seeing her sisters act.

"I don't mind at all."

Now walking backwards, Honey Mae was still collecting memory photographs. Playfully biting her bottom lip, she gave him a wink spun around and began running up the slanted hill to the school house.

"Hey, Ms. Jackson," screaming at the top of his lungs. "You forgot to ask me my name."

"No I didn't!" she shouted back, standing in the school house door.

"It's Mitch! Mitch Purify!"

She pretended she didn't hear him as she disappeared behind the door. He sat there for a few moments shaking his head. He gave a hefty whip of the reins to govern the horse to move forward. "Getty-up."

Speaking out loud he said, "We will meet again sweet lady and that's a promise."

He didn't see her peeping from behind the door watching him. She watched him until he faded into the distance. Even then she watched the whirlwind of dust his horse and buggy created until it cleared. The students that started arriving at school, wondered what she was watching but dared not ask, not even her sisters.

The next day, racing from home to see him, she became fearful when time began to slip away and he was nowhere to be found. "*Had I said something to offend him?*" She wondered.

She stopped to re-lace her shoes six times trying to stall time. Still not hearing the familiar sound she heard each morning, she was disappointed as second by second she heard nothing but cackling children, playing and talking on their way to school.

She had reached the end of the path where she turned to go up the hill to school. Kneeling down one more time, she suddenly heard the sweet gallop that made her smile. A smile so bright, it was hard to separate it from the sunlight. Her toes were curling. Oh how she was excited, just knowing her pleasure was trotting along in an old trash wagon that opened the treasures of her heart.

Inside of her, a symphony of music played the strings to her soul. Strangely, she was inflamed with never felt before desires—desires for his aroma, the taste of his breath. She yearned to lean on his timber wide muscles that flexed to their own rhythm and aching to build memories filled with laughter shared together. Inhaling the thought of him escalated her sexual height without ever engaging in the actual act itself.

His presence chipped away at her stone cold heart as she released the tension that housed itself inside of her for many years. Her body began to release a strange yet pleasurable satisfaction. The closest she had ever come to being with a man was when she slipped on a pair of her father's trousers he had taken off and she began playing in them.

She, smiling and acting coy, turned to greet the deep voice.

"Good morning sweet lady. You don't know how much you brighten my day by just seeing you again."

How well she knew. The evidence was in her panties.

"Sweet lady, I tried to call out to you yesterday before you disappeared, trying to tell you my name. The name is Mitchell, Mitchell Purify, but you can name me whatever you like."

She dared not tell him, she heard every word. She had even rehearsed his last name with hers, *"Honey Mae Purify, yes that sounds great."*

Stepping down from his wagon, she never imagined he was so tall. 6'4" tall, compared to her 5'3" stature.

She didn't want him to come too close, fearing he would sense in her, the rage of her hormones.

"Damn, you're tall," she blurted out. *"With big hands,"* she thought.

"Too much for you?" He asked.

"Only if you don't give me a chance." She flirted, glaring deep into his eyes.

"Little lady, I'm not sure what you're talking about or thinking, but you can have whatever you want."

Then he licked his lips right before he gently placed them on hers. She allowed him a few moments before pushing him away. Not wanting to, but she had become self conscious of the possible aroma her body was sending out from her underwear.

"I'm sorry, did I do something wrong?" He asked.

"See you later Mitch." Deliberately not answering his questions keeping him wondering.

"You sure will," he said.

Once in the school, she went straight out the back door, hoping for time before the school bell rang. She went behind some bushes, sat down on the ground, crossed one leg tightly across the other soon realizing what she was feeling was; an orgasm.

CHAPTER 9

Sitting here I remembered when mama told the story about . . . .

More than two weeks went by and she hadn't seen Mitch. Her concerns really grew, just like her feelings. Down on herself, she pondered many thoughts. Sometimes her thoughts were coupled with anger, loss of appetite and lack of sleep.

"What did I do?

What did I say?

Did I come on too strong?

Curse too much?

Could he smell my raging hormones?

Was that a turn off?"

Angered, she said aloud, "screw him, if that smell ran him away, he must be a sissy. I hate him!"

Her aunt was worried about her sudden mood change, but constantly told her that each day things would get better. She knew Callie meant well, but she'd rather be alone and work her way through this hurt. Callie and Fodie worried about her, but respected her wishes.

Meanwhile, instead of the hard sharecropping that had drained and taken the life out of his father, Mitch decided he would have his business work for him and not his business working the life out of him. His goal was to send William and Johannah to school to complete their education, the same school where he met Honey Mae three weeks before their father's death, a young lady that he thought he would probably never see again because losing his father made life with his sister and brother more demanding.

At the same time Honey Mae was having her own troubles . . .

The day began with a beautiful bright sunshine, the sky dressed in powder blue and the clouds hung like white drapes. The breeze from the wind was so gentle you could almost hear its secrets whispered in your ears.

Disenchanted with school, the only thing Honey accomplished each day was perfect attendance. Surprisingly, however, on this particular day, her focus was given to the front of the class when she saw her parents Charity and Jack standing at the threshold of the schoolhouse door. The teacher went over to greet them. Immediately she knew something was wrong because sadness covered their faces.

Honey Mae thought they had come to school to talk about something she had done or maybe something Lucille or Mabel had done, but quickly expelled that thought. Mabel and Lucille were their parents favorite children and could do no wrong.

She approached them with much hesitation after the teacher called her to the front of the class, because she was listening for one of her sister's names to be called instead of hers. Instantly her stomach turned into butterflies and her mind skipped to possible attempted murder charges on the attempt of her father's life. Thinking to herself, *"Why in the hell are my parents coming to get me instead of the police?"*

Charity extended her arms, with tears rolling down her face, to receive her child but found coldness and the coldness became greater when she made eye contact with her father.

As she arrived at the desk, "Ma'am?" she said with her arms folded tightly against her body.

Embarrassed at her child's surprising reaction, Charity placed her arms down at here sides.

Jack greeted her verbally, saying gently, "Hi baby?"

Her eyes told him the story of the words she wanted to say. With a sharp piercing look she said to herself, *"How dare this son of a bitch form a word like baby and say it to me?"*

"Honey Mae", the teacher said "your parents need to speak with you."

Continuing her inward conversation, Honey Mae thought, *"I wish you would tell them get the hell away from the school and me and take their phony tears with them".*

She just stood there without a word. Charity grabbed her by her shoulders with force causing Honey Mae to turn so they could be face to face. Tears now rolling heavily down her face her mouth became dry after looking into her daughter's eyes. Quickly, she looked away not being able to tell her the bad news.

Ms. Gibbs, Honey Mae's teacher, tried to intervene and said, "Would you like to go outside to talk to your child; you may need the pri . . . ."

Cutting off her words, "Whatever they need to say, they can say it right here," Honey Mae quickly responded.

Jack took control of the situation, but not in the manner of which he made his trademark; this time he tried to treat it as a loving father. Standing close in front of her, he placed his hands on her shoulders.

She looked over at his left hand, turned her head looking at his right hand; then she looked into his face and snatched herself away, saying, "You said you had something to say, now spit it out."

Her behavior did not deter her father's affection. Once again placing his hands on her shoulders, he held on.

"Listen to me," he said, "we need to go outside."

"What's all this, 'we need to go outside' mess, just tell me."

Sadly he said, "We have something to tell you about Callie and Fodie."

The stone face that she had displayed became relaxed after hearing the name Callie and Fodie. Her father had peeked her interest and had all of her attention.

"What about Aunt Callie and Uncle Fodie?" She asked nervously.

"Let's go outside." Her mother said softly.

"We've already covered that outside territory so tell me here and now, right now, got damn it." Viciously she said.

"Honey Mae Jackson, you watch your mouth." Charity said raising her voice.

"It's ok." Jack said, almost whispering his words looking in his daughter's face.

"There was a fire at the house while Callie had bedded down for a nap and Fodie was outside working. A neighbor ran over screaming 'Fire!' When Fodie looked up, smoke was coming from the house. Fodie ran inside trying to save Callie, the fire became so great neither made it out. They were both trapped inside."

At first Honey Mae just stood there staring into space with no reaction as the other students watched, knowing the news was not good. When all of a sudden overcome by devastation after hearing the news, she screamed with hysterics and bolted out the door.

She ran down the hill onto the dirt road into the direction of the home of Callie and Fodie's. Chasing her down, Jack seized his distraught daughter. Scooping her into his arms, he embraced her as she fell limp, Charity, Lucille and Mabel a few feet behind them, were completely out of breath after following the chase.

Charity looked toward heaven and said, "Thank you God." The children and the teacher cheered and clapped in the background knowing Honey Mae was safe.

Later that night when she woke, she thought she had been dreaming, but quickly realized she wasn't. The room was dark, as she got out of bed stretching her arms out in front of her feeling for any obstacles that may be blocking her way or could cause a possible accident. Finally reaching the light switch, she turned it on and as she looked around everything looked familiar, too familiar for her, knowing everything all too well. She was in her old room in her parents' home.

"How long have I been asleep?" She wondered.

Thinking hard, the last thing she remembered was Charity telling Dr. Buggs, *"Thank you."* And him responding *". . . and that sedative I gave her should keep her quiet and resting for a while."*

Honey Mae, having no where else to go, hated to acknowledge the fact that she had no control of her life and forced to reside in the home of her father, Watkin Jackson, she became angry with God.

Feeling trapped, like a mouse with no hole for an exit, sitting on the side of her bed, she took in a deep breath not wanting to exhale hoping death would come quickly before needing the next gulp of air. It didn't work. She felt doomed to a tragic sentence, life along side two sisters she never had a relationship with, a father she tried to kill and a mother that had turned against her. She vowed to keep them at bay by never displaying kindness or formulating words to represent anything but an invitation out of her space and life.

There was only one consolation to this cruel trick fate had placed upon her. It helped her deal with her loneliness by rebuilding the broken down connection that once bonded her and her mother, Charity. In the past, she had allowed others to be aware of the deep emotions she carried for her mother, conveying it dearly with statements and words like, 'my sweet Charity' showing her natural and unscripted love for her mother. How deeply she needed her but didn't know how to tell her without looking weak. She thought weakness was a human flaw. She needed her for everything to help her with the business of the things left behind for her by Callie and Fodie.

Everything they owned was left for Honey's future, all that wasn't consumed by the fire. However, didn't any of this really matter to Honey Mae. As far as she was concerned, it could all be given away if she could have her uncle and aunt back. Realizing this would never happen, she wept.

Early the next day with little sleep, she sat up in the bed recalling something important her Uncle Fodie said to her and Callie, but something Callie already knew, *"Lil lady, I'm 'bout ta tell ya a bit of news dat neva fell on utta ears befo', 'sides my plum pudding Callie, 'cause dis wife of mine can hol' yo' bidness lac' bidness 'spose ta be hol'. I be neva worried 'bout nobody else tongue waggin' 'round town telling what dey thank dey 'no 'bout yo' biiness. I needs ta feel de same 'bout'cha. Can I count on ya Honey Mae?"*

Excited to be a part of his trust, she quickly said, *"Yes sir, uncle Fodie, you can count on me."*

"Wells I ain't put my trus' in mankind dey change too much ta keep up wit' deys thanking, deys can be lo' down and uttawise. So I do's an' put my bankin' in a large metal box out back in da shed. It's unda dat small roll of hay I props

my heel on, de one dat look lac' a footstool. Do ya know de one I's talking 'bout?"

"Yes sir I do." Sounding excited

"I change dat roll of hay of'en, rollin one away an' rollin annuta in, I do's dat ta cover de big hole an' in dat hole is where I do my bankin. I be da bes' damn banka you and Mama (another one of his pet names for Callie) can count on an' trus'. I's trus' nobody fo' long, but I's trus' ya'll fo' a lifetime. Everythang I work fo' wuz fo' Callie, now it's fo' de both of ya."

"Ain't dat a weight off da mind," Callie said, *"telling us lac' you gon' die, you ain't goin' nowhere, Heaven ain't ready fo' ya and I refuse ta give Hell po'mission ta thank it can have ya, so you ain't goin' nowhere."* Callie raised her voice. Then she began to chuckle out loud and everyone joined in together in hardy laughter.

By this time Honey's memories had become too great and she left the hay rolling for another day. Her body started a slight but uncontrollable tremor as she cried even more.

Producing a very loud shrill, she looked toward heaven and said, "WHY! I needed aunt Callie and uncle Fodie more than you God, so tell me what do I do now?" Using God at her disposal. Bringing her eyes back down to the floor, she just stood there, helpless and defenseless.

Dressed in a white skirt and navy blue blouse, both freshly starched just like Callie would do them, she fell to her knees giving no thought to getting dirty; she just didn't care, her pain was great.

Soon gathering her composure, she headed off to school, wanting to quit but she forged ahead knowing this would make Callie and Fodie proud. Walking toward the school and wiping away the tears, a colorful vision ran through her head. She could imagine seeing her aunt in the kitchen cooking up a storm, causing a tantalizing aroma to fill the house of fried chicken and biscuits. She could hear her call out for her to come down and fill her belly with loving pleasure. Running down the stairs, she found uncle Fodie leaning back in his favorite chair already at the kitchen table with his fork and knive in hand.

She was always afraid that chair may break under pressure. She could hear her uncle Fodie telling aunt Callie while sitting there in his overalls, *"Dis sum'n' ta eat jus tickled my nose rhat off my face 'cause it sho' mo' good, I gots ta tie my tongue ta keep from swallowing it."* Her tears disappeared and were replaced with a joyful surge of laughter that was much needed to feel better.

Suddenly she heard an old but familiar sound. She was confused as to whether to be confused or angry or to keep on smiling. Most of all she was hoping it wasn't an overactive imagination because she had become anxious. The familiar sound was horse hooves pounding away on the ground. With no doubt, she knew that it was the tall handsome man named Mitch Purify without even turning around. Again, using God at her disposal, she prayed, *"Please let it be him."*

The anticipation was overwhelming as she waited filled with desperate question, questions such as, *"why did he disappear, why had so much time passed since the last time they saw each other?"*

She knew in her heart that she could not be married to a man that would just disappear without notice, rhyme or reason. She knew she cared for him because he continued to linger in her life and heart. Without speaking, she always hoped with every moment of each day that his mental presence from her would soon evaporate, leaving no sign of him ever being present in her life. Unsuccessful in this fruitless mind game of trying to forget him, instead she welcomed his vast approach. Suddenly an arousing feeling came over her; she just wanted to look into his eyes. Disappointment would shatter her world if the horse that was clopping behind her was not his steed. God heard her plea, as the voice from the wagon commanded the horses to yield to a one word sound, "Whoa!"

The galloping sound that the horses carried came to a slow and eventually a complete halt. "Hello little lady, it's good to see you again," he said quickly and nervously.

He dared not to ask how she was doing. The question would lead to too wide of an opening for a possible angry woman to come in and he wasn't sure if he were ready to be that patient. She turned, looked into his eyes and her knees almost gave away. She said "Well sir it's great to see you also."

"You headed to school quite early this morning aren't you?"

"Couldn't sleep, so I got dressed and headed out early to get a jump on all the education that I could consume today."

He laughed a very distinctive but genuine sound of welcomed amusement. "Beautiful and funny too, what more can you ask for?" He said.

"Yeah, what more?" turning the humorous and glorious moment into a windfall of seriousness.

"For some reason, pretty lady, I felt a little chill behind that last line you delivered."

"Really?"

"Now I know there's a strong coldness in the air."

Silence gathered between them and danced with the singing and the sweet chirping of the birds in the far distance. The night before had been swallowed up with treacherous high winds and engaging itself with the threat of dangerous thunder storms. However, the heavens promptly calmed the angry atmosphere and instead extended quiet and peace. But the morning was flooded with a hot and early stream of sunshine that soaked up the dew that dripped onto the grass as the daylight slept and the night stood guard. The sun slowly removed the moisture so new growth could spring up and evolve into a healthy meadow that created beauty surrounding all by its natural wonders. The sun luminously wrapped its blanket around trees, shrubs and flowers as they stood tall saluting with appreciation.

Honey, unaware, not caring about God's creation, was inside of herself, feeling only for herself. Unable to contain herself, she spoke with a voice of authority, "How dare you come riding up on your horse and think that you could have a normal conversation with me and not give an explanation as to why I haven't seen you?" Hostility was hurdled all over the place.

"Little lady, I don't think anything could be normal with you."

Looking toward him with a look of disdain, she said, "How dare you try and insult me with your got damn judgment."

He replied, "Listen little lady, you don't know who the hell I am right now, so you are going to have to take your damn ass on down the road before I say something I don't mean to a lady and believe me if I say it, I won't have any regrets." He never allowed his voice to elevate or escalate out of control, but his statement was firm.

"I'll go on down the road, but I won't go before I decide to go." She rebuked.

She stood there with her knuckles on her hips looking at him with a cold and heartless stare. Pausing, he looked way, before returning his attention to her. Then he said, "Not feeling like I owe you an explanation, but I'm going to give you one anyway." Taking in a deep breath, he released it with a long and loud sigh. "I haven't been around because, (pausing) my family has been in a state of emergency."

Her look was disengaging. Enduring her lack luster cheer he carried on his crusade of words waging against her defense.

"My father's illness took us by surprise and his death even more shocking," he started.

Her look went from stone to almost sympathetic.

He continued, "Leaving me to care for my sister and brother, Hannah and Willie. We have no mother; our mother died at the birth of Hannah and my father did all he could, even during his sickness, taking care of Hannah, Willie and myself."

Trying to remain composed he took in another breath. "They're old enough mostly to take care of themselves and as you can see I do a good job of taking care of myself, but it made my father feel worthy and proud to see us through, even in the end when he just sat in his chair all day. To us he was the greatest man that ever lived."

Still sitting in his wagon towering over Honey Mae, he bowed his head and at that moment his words made Honey Mae take complete notice; words nor sentiment could she ever find inside or include about her father.

Mitch could see the melting of ice and the removing of septum that had been dividing them at the beginning of his story. Honey remained quiet, holding her books close to chest, she became quite concerned. Engulfing and inhaling the information like and anaconda crushing its victim before swallowing them whole, Mitch continued to share the days gone by.

"In his last days or should I say weeks, not only was our father bedridden, but he lost his dignity. I had to take care, with the help of Willie and Hannah, treating our father in the manner of a baby." Unable to control the tears any longer, they trickled down his cheek. Honey's admiration for him heightened. "We buried him a few weeks ago, alongside our mother."

Pulling a handkerchief from the back pocket of his overalls, he wiped his face erasing the evidence of his tears. "I had to start working on my trash route earlier than usual during that time, returning home at noonday while Hannah and Willie were in school. I fed and cared for him before leaving him alone again. This part of the day always made me sad when I had to leave my father, but I was glad to know he was in God's care. There were a lot of late evenings, some of them were late nights after taking care of my business, I'd come home to do chores that needed to be done."

Once again, Honey's selfishness stepped in as she started to think, *"What the hell did Hannah and Willie do?"*

Before the thought could be finished, he said and answering her unasked question, "Hannah and Willie tend their books; their concentration on study was and is a strict rule in our family. It holds the greatest weight following love. Chores never came before education, my father and mother would always say, and now I say the same."

Honey felt awful for the corroded thinking she was doing and wondered if this man could read minds or had psychic abilities. Years later, she would learn that many people had already stomped the life out of that question causing him to be on guard prepared with firmness in answering the question before it could be proposed.

"So little lady, if that wasn't a good enough response as to why I wanted to have a normal, decent conversation with you ma'am, I'm sorry." At this point Mitch began to raise his voice, "So before I take my ass down the road little lady, you can keep yours in the air and learn some manners," placing much emphasis on his statement.

Not allowing her the opportunity to utter another word, he slapped the reins down on the horses back and yelled, "Yigh!"

The horses sped off and fled down the dusty, dry trail leaving a smoky cloud of dust shadowing her view of the man she had declared to be her husband right out of her life, maybe forever. Once the mass of earthy powder cleared, she was left with only her thoughts, rethinking on her unwarranted drama.

"You damn bitch!" Exclaiming a self description, *"I wish I could kick myself square in the ass."* This time she lowered her head; it was almost as low as her spirit. She began an inward war, discovering her behavior didn't accomplish a thing.

Announcing to herself, she vowed to recover and not let this great possibility of marriage be decayed due to her lose and foul mouth. She said out loud, "Your ass belongs to me, Mitch Purify."

CHAPTER 10

Honey Mae's attention at school and home in the many weeks to come grew increasingly worse. Many accredited her and excused her behavior to the loss of her aunt and uncle, and no one dared to discipline or try to correct her neurotic and sometimes irrational conduct. Mabel, Lucille and even Jack steered clear of the storm that was brewing inside of her.

Charity, however, saw the pain growing in her daughter and knew her problem but not the solution. She was in love just as much as she was hurting from the demise of Fodie and Callie. Knowing it was deep, Charity would only give Honey a smile and walk away, she would not invite herself in. She wanted to be invited and welcomed.

A few times, while Charity was sitting in her chair knitting or needle pointing, Honey Mae would come over to the rocker where she was sitting, kneel down beside her and place her head on her mother's knee. Charity would place her work on the table next to her and place her hand on her child's head. No words were spoken or exchanged and neither was an explanation needed.

Each morning Honey Mae set out for school earlier than the day before. She became anxious as she grew into a lady in waiting—waiting to capture a certain game that had sassy charm. Time went by, but there were no horse hooves pounding the ground, no rickety wagon sounds approaching from behind and no sign of the man that held her heart.

Words Mitch had said to her rang in her head, the words being the only reason she still attended school. *"Education was important to my father and mother, making it important to me."*

She continued in her education because she made up in her mind that she never wanted to disappoint Mitch ever again, even if she hated school. After class each day, on their way home, Lucille and Mabel walked slowly alongside their sister with great concern. No matter how Honey treated them, they genuinely loved and cared about her well being. Keeping quiet, Mabel gathered the courage to put her arms around Honey's shoulders when she started to cry. She was happy to give consolation, but surprised Honey didn't reject her advance.

Eventually Charity explained to the girls what was happening to their sister, but even Charity became more and more concerned about the lack of eating and weight loss that plagued her child.

One day Charity went into Honey's room after they arrived home from school to speak with her, without knocking, Charity entered into her bedroom swiftly and said, "Honey, we need to talk." Sitting on the bed next to her as she lay there sobbing, "You've got to get a grip on things baby, or we'll lose you too."

"Tell me how?" She asked, while crying profusely.

"I really don't know how, but we've got to come up with something."

Honey sat up.

The room was beautifully decorated in yellow and white. The bedroom furniture was oak that had been painted white and the curtains were in yellow eyelet fabric with the bedspread to match. Charity had admiration for how Honey and Mabel always kept their room, so tidy and neat, but Lucille had room for great change; she was a slob.

Placing her arm around her daughter, causing Honey to lay her head on her mother's shoulder, "What will we think of?" Honey inquired.

"Let's start with telling me his name."

Surprised by Charity's knowledge of something she never told but quickly answered, "Mitchell Purify, but I call him Mitch."

"Well let me say this, there is no one answer to a century old problem; there just isn't. The only suggestion that I have is . . . . ," Charity pausing, "that you're going to get up from feeling sorry for yourself and we're going to go and have some fun. We're going out on a scavenger hunt."

Honey's expression had question marks written all over it. She was curious as to what her mother was talking about.

"Remember telling me about possible treasure you have on your property, underneath a rolled up footstool I believe."

Honey laughed out loud.

"What's so funny?' Charity asked.

"It's sounds funny to hear anyone say 'your property', and you'll be surprised at the footstool."

"Oh, yeah?" Now the question mark was on Charity's face.

"Your property, your treasure, and I guess we'll be going hunting on that property today." Playfully slapping her daughter on the thigh, she said, "Now get up and let's go."

Grabbing her shoes, she put them on her feet; she joined her mother as they ran downstairs like two girls laughing and giggling. "We're out!" Charity shouted as they headed out the door.

Honey was shocked that her mother didn't flinch or seem to care what her father would say or do. At the same time she caught a glimpse of Lucille and Mabel's faces smiling. They were happy to hear their sister's laughter; whatever their mother did, worked and there was no room for jealousy. They also knew at this point in time that emotion would not be tolerated by Charity.

Arriving at the rubble and ashes where the house once stood, they saw that the only thing still standing was the chimney. They headed around back to the shed. At first Charity had thought she had made a mistake, forgetting that this scene could upset her daughter. But to her surprise she was still giggling with adventure.

Opening the door to the shed or the "banking institution" as uncle Fodie would call it, would turn out to be his grandest idea, saving the money from the fire. When they found the box, it was filled with Callie's fine jewelry, beads, I.O.U's people owed Fodie and hundreds and hundreds of dollars.

"I'm rich!" Honey screamed as she kneeled down on the ground holding her treasure.

"Not quite," her mother said.

"Well almost."

"Not there either, but you have a nice juicy nest egg."

"Well at least let me pretend I have two nest eggs."

"I can do humor," Charity said as she nodded with a smile and feeling good while rubbing her fingers over her daughter's hair.

"This is good. This is your secret Honey Mae and this is your money. You and you alone will decide what you will do with it and how you will spend it."

"But you know Charity."

"And as far as anyone else I don't know," playfully she said, "let's pinky swear." She extended her baby finger out for Honey to latch on to.

Honey paused with surprise because for the first time in her life, Charity felt like her best friend, more than her mother. She was the greatest confidante anyone could ever ask for.

As she pinky swore with her mother she said, "I don't understand, but if you're okay then it's okay by me." She refrained from questioning her mother's motives and advice because it was always good except the advice about her father.

They bagged up the tin box in an old burlap sack Charity grabbed from the front porch when they ran out of the house. Honey placed some of the money in her pocket and the rest stayed in the box. They found a new hiding place closer to home where Charity allowed Honey to be the only one to know where the new burial place was located. After that day, they never talked about the box again. However, Honey visited and examined it often.

During this time, Jack's sister Tessie died and her two girls came to town to live with the Jackson Family. Their names were Tomorrow and Charity. Tessie loved the name Charity so much she asked permission to name her expectant child after Jack's wife, if it was a girl.

While Tessie was sick, she made arrangements for Charity to live with Jack and Tomorrow to live with their cousin Stoney. Tomorrow and Charity were upset to be separated but Stoney and Jack each had their hands filled with their own families and thought that each should share responsibilities.

After a short period, Charity realized how unhappy she had become, not only because of the death of her mother but also how mean she was treated by Honey Mae. She was angry because the only chance she thought that she had was the sympathy Honey would feel because of her loss, but that was to no avail. Instantly Honey hated Charity because of the intrusion and living arrangements causing Charity to become self reliant.

Charity found herself having to hide bread from breakfast and meat from dinner in order to have enough to eat. There was food given to her, but Honey Mae threatened her if she consumed it.

CHAPTER 11

After forty years and during the course of my grandmother's illness, I came to know my Aunt Charity, the lady named after my great grandmother. Aunt Charity told me the story of . . . .

Living life with Uncle Jack's family was terrible; however, my first mistake was to ask the wrong question, asking her something she had already said, "Was life terrible living there?" The frail lady I had come to know, with a soft voice, looking apprehensive brought thunder along with her response.

"YES!" Lifting the sound of her voice, "I already told you life wuz terrible, but terrible ain't de description for what I went through. Living hell is the description and even hell don't give a good description of the crap I ate. "Speaking of eating . . ." she recalled, "I won't allowed to eat, Honey Mae saw to that." She seemed excited to tell me this history or it could have just been her memory working well.

Looking down at her wrinkled hands that were worn with time, twining them together over and over in a wringing type motion, she told stories, with sometimes broken English, that made my mouth open and my eyes become wide. I listened and said not a word.

Aunt Charity continued her compelling stories . . . .

"Honey Mae had made up in her mind that she really didn't want the country girl living with them, but if I had to, there was no way that she would allow me to be equal to them. She had to show me that I was in Honeyville Land. She said things like, "I couldn't eat with them because I couldn't hold a fork properly and that I smacked whenever I put food in my mouth. So I tried to eat and talk proper like them so Honey won't be so mean." However, Aunt Charity spoke, seemingly very conscious, in a slow southern drawl.

She was a proud, tall, stocky woman with thin legs; her face always seemed sad, her heart heavy and her eyes trapped pain so deep inside till there was no way out. There was no way she could find within herself to elude her past. However, the pictures arranged around the room of her house reflected her as once being quite pretty as she stood towering over her family in the photos including Uncle Rufus, her husband.

After a minute she said, "The memories that should haunt Honey Mae never will, she's too mean to get scared in her head. She's yo' grandmamma and I didn't know you existed till Mitch Junior died a year ago. And you be grown then. Me and Tomorrow didn't know and Willie didn't know either, cause he sho' woulda told his wife, my sustah, since Willie and Mitch be brothers. So evil Honey didn't never tell no one 'bout you, kept you hid. I found out she be shame of you through gossip." Chuckling.

Aunt Charity's words hurt. I already knew what she said was true, but I didn't let her know how it still affected me. Then she went on with her story.

"Yeah, yo' grandma bragged at Mitch Junior's funeral, but we calls him Junior, on how good you took care of her and hope her out with her ailments, taking her to the doctor and all that kind of carrying on."

In my mind I felt somewhat upset wondering if my grandmother had given people the impression she was using me, but on the other hand it really didn't matter. I did it because I cared and found the humor in it. Inadvertently, I laughed out loud. Aunt Charity gave me a strange look, looking as though she thought I was crazy for laughing out of the clear blue sky.

Quickly I apologized, "I'm sorry Aunt Charity; I just thought of something funny."

"Well I hope it wasn't me that you find funny," she said.

"No, no, no, it wasn't about you; you just jarred my memory concerning my grandmother . . ." Before I could I finish, she started telling more stories of my infamous grandmother.

"Honey was a pissta' packin' mean-spirited bitch. When she got grown I's memba' when she gots married, that dang fool husband of hurs, Mitch bought hur a .38 pistol and regretted it after she shot at him a couple of times, and she shot at a few other folk. I knows this man that lost his gun around the same time Mitch brought this .38 home and gives it to Honey. But he sho' shoulda kept the bullets when he gave hur that gun 'cause a gun can't work wit' no bullets. It woulda saved him from a shot in the ass."

My eyes increased in size, I was filled with curiosity. Not sure if she was saying that my grandmother had shot someone, I asked with intrigue. "Did anyone ever get shot by my grandmother?"

"Sho', she shot Prentuss Hall in the ass and leg. His ass heal, but he lost his leg. Put'ner don' shot that leg plum off, left it dangling on the limb by a strang o' meat. Sho' was a sight to place yo' eyes on, so bad a sight his eyes gave way to a fainting spell, when they took him to the hospital; he stayed sleep a few days after the leg was took off. We don't know if he stayed sleep cause the operation or the faintin' spell. And chile we don't know what they did wit that leg. He shoulda kept it and beat the hell outta Honey wit it."

I started giggling. My mind became jammed with questions, two at a time. I couldn't keep up with the questions. There were so many I was confused as to what to ask next. I decided on the question, "Did she go to jail?"

"Hell naw, she ain't go no jail; she shoulda gon' and rot in there. Damn if that ol' fool didn't press no charges. Said it was an accident; I might could understand the leg getting' into an accident but the ass? Come on? Back then the po'lice ain't care 'bout no black mane, they don't care 'bout no black mane now. So they ain't investigate nuttin', case closed."

Suddenly Aunt Charity seemed to drift away from her thoughts for a short period, rambling in non connective short sentences, sometimes forgetting my presence. But never did she change her demeanor or the stride in which she tells her story.

Traveling back down the highway of memory lane, she blurted out, "He sho' was Honey's damn fool, a fool 'til he died. Yeah," pausing, "that sorry case was closed."

She was sitting there with her arms folded across her chest, her flowered cotton dress with short sleeves that seemed too tight around the arms and shoulders, possibly cutting off her circulation. However, the tightness didn't seem to bother her, moving her arms freely at all times.

"I wish that grandma' of yo's hadda gon' to jail; maybe she woulda find out she wasn't so tough. But that was then and this is now. She got old like me but I calls her on the phone often to check up on her. I don' gon' on to fo'given'. Anyways I got too old to whup her ass."

Squeezing her folded arms more securely across her chest, she released a sound that sounded like a faint chuckle accompanied by a great sigh of relief, a relief to talk about this ugly part of her life.

"She be too old and weak now to pick up that .38 let 'lone shoot it. Now that's funny," she chuckled again. "Only thang she shoot off now is her big ass mouth." Her chuckles turned into an obvious laughter that was infectious even to me. We laughed for at least a minute.

Wiping the tears from her face and trying to gather herself, she said, "Yo' grandmama," she turned looking at me, "you know what? That kinda sound funny, Honey Mae a grandmama, and you's be a pretty yung thang. And know what, you look jus like Lucille. You knows that Honey Mae's baby sustah was a pretty gurl, a beautiful gurl. Yo' grandma was pretty but hur stick didn't stand tall like Lucille. She had hips that made the wind talk and those tight skirts pop like a drum major's whistle when she walk. She gyrated her hips from east to west. Her waist was so tiny everythang hads to be altered fo' her to wear. Chile, don't mention her prize winnin legs."

Telling me this, she slapped her own knee still laughing. "All the men folk, 'cluding married ones was drooling on their wives when they sees her. I guess they couldn't help theyself, they thought they was single at that particular moment. Them women folks hated her, but loved her cause she was so friendly."

Aunt Charity placed massive amounts of emphasis on these words of Aunt Lucille being friendly. "She really was sho' good to me. That is when Honey wasn't lookin'. Them sisters was 'fraid of Honey. I 'member when Lucille once eased and give me a pair of shoes to wear for one day but when I finally put them on so I could go and see my kinfolk; they was too shawt.

I didn't know that old buzzard Honey was watchin me, jus to start some crap. Old Honey started yelling out to Aunt Charity that I stol'em. Lucille was gon', I beleeved she woulda spoke up and told the truth. But Aunt Charity beleeved Honey and made me wore them shoes wit my feet folded at the toe. I was mad at Honey but I was mo' mad at Aunt Charity for beleevin' I stole. You know I beleeve she dies thankin' that to. I cried that day, but I cried fo' my po' feet cause they hurt. I guess I was hurt two times, my foots and Aunt Charity."

Hearing her say 'Aunt Charity' made me stop because to me she was Aunt Charity. "Did you continue wearing the shoes after that day, Aunt Charity?" I asked. Another faint chuckled presented itself.

"Naw, chile, I didn't."

"Well what happened to the shoes?"

"Well, when I gots back Aunt Charity made me giv 'em back."

"Give them back?" I questioned.

"Sho' she did. Aunt Charity was a good person, sweet. Took a lot of crap from Uncle Jack that she shouldn't and even worsa, damn problems from that bitch chile of theirs Honey. Trying nots to hurt my feelings, Aunt Charity knowed those shoes was too shawt, so to punish me she won't let me have 'em, she took 'em back. Aunt Charity knew that punishment would make me happy.

Yo' grandmama wanted her to beat me."

"Aunt Charity, you said you no longer hated my grandmother, but when you speak, I get the feeling hate still lurks inside you."

Looking up from whirling the wedding band she continued to wear around her finger, she stared into my eyes once again, with her eyebrow arched. Her next words were as gentle as her words were slow, almost making time seem to just melt away before she spoke.

"Baby, I'm not trying to make up any good or bad feelings for what I don' said and how I don' said it don't mean a thang. I forgave Honey long time ago. But her lowdown ways stuck in my memories. They be bedded down wit' me everyday of my life. Them thangs she don', even she can't forget."

In her continued pursuit to share her pain, hours passed. Sometimes during that course of time, nothing was said. We watched television in between or she simply hummed with the tune being played on the radio softly in the background, and sometime she interrupted her private solitude by telling another story.

"I member coming up to Birmingham from the country all excited to be part of Uncle Jack's 'phisticated and sweet family, instead I got pissed on. I worked harder than I ever had, I was a maid. Washin', cookin', workin' the field and pickin up behind them sorry asses. Most times it was done outta spite by you know who and jus natural by Lucille. Po' thang, she just don't keep house good. But Aunt Charity and Lucille hope much as they could without Uncle Jack and Honey knowing what's goin on. Mabel stay much to herself."

Suddenly, catching a second breath and changing the subject, Aunt Charity said, "Stand up! Stand up so's I can get a good look at you chile," reaching out and grabbing as though she was going to give some assistance to my standing up from the sofa.

Once I stood up she said, "Yeah you made up jus like her 'cept fo' them legs. You's win second prize fo' yo' legs. Yo' grandmama win furst prize and Lucille would get the grand prize. Lucille was in God's special gift givin' race."

I took all things that she said in stride, I knew she meant no harm, as a matter of fact, I think she was giving a compliment in her own special way. One thing was for sure, she was truly related to my grandmother because she didn't hold back her words.

She continued talking, "Ya'll blessed in the face, body, ass and legs department, 'cept you a little shy on legs."

Still playing with the ring on her finger, her face seemed to be invaded by sadness. I began wondering if the ring was a troubling factor in her life. I began thinking 'was this the original ring that her husband placed on her finger?' I didn't want to start the subject of her husband until later in our conversation. So I gently touched her on her knee to arouse her from her trance that had taken over her thoughts.

So I said, "When I look at the pictures you have around this room, you caught a lot of bees with your honey; and looking at you now you still have that same honey." Gently, I shoved her on the shoulder and said, "You were a good looking woman then and you are a good looking woman now."

"G'won somewhere chile. Wit' my looks I just caught the bee and he stung my black ass, lookin fo' sum Honey."

"Were you ever married?"

"I neva said I won't marry. He's the bee wit the tweeder that I got stung wit'. But he was no count. But he played 'round my honeycomb and got my black ass pregnant and we's got married. It was rotten from the start, but we's stayed married til' he died. He lived mean, he died mean. Even dead I know's he still be the same. He did hope give me two boys." The giggles showed up again. "I gon' through hell mos my life after my ma' and pa' left dis world. Tomorrow's life was caught up in God's safety net. Our cousin Stoney treated her real good. She was no maid, she wore no shoes that was too shawt and married a good man, yo' Uncle Willie. Yeah, Willie was a good man."

Aunt Charity seemed to repeat a lot of her statements as though giving confirmation.

"Were you ever jealous of your sister's living situation?"

"Lawd a' mercy, No! I's neva be jealous of my susta blessed fo'chun. I jus wish sometimes I had a little chunk of it to keep in my hope chest. But I know if God had put her in my place she would be gon' past dead the furst day. God knows I could live through it and He knows I won't like it, but He knows I'd do betta than my susta living in Uncle Jack house."

"Which one of you is the oldest, Aunt Charity?"

"Chile that don't make no never mind. Which one of us look the oldest?"

"Uhh, Uhh." I started babbling, she put me on the spot, I didn't want to insult anyone.

"See what I mean chile. I'm sittin' here waitin' on you to tell me what matter that be. Anyway I'll answer yo' lil silly question. I be the ol'est. We have one year 'tween us. See chile, in life when the end come, you might understand how it ain't important how old you be."

I thought to myself, *"I guess day by day, little by little, I'm learning more and more of what's important and what isn't."* Aunt Charity caused my memory to roll back over things I had heard many times over the course of my life, like, 'age ain't nothing but a number', I did not want to ask anything that might offend Aunt Charity so I waited a few seconds before I injected my next question.

Patting her hands, I said, "Aunt Charity."

Without hesitation she responded, "Yes baby."

When she said that I strayed from my next question to tell her, "I love it when you say that, 'Yes baby'; it sounds so warm."

She smiled and placed her hand on top of mine. Returning to my question I asked, "Would you please tell me more about Aunt Lucille and tee Mabel?"

'Let me fetch us sumttin to drink furst 'cause I made us some lemonade. It's not as good as it used to be cause my hands ol' and weak. But it still sho' mo' good e'nuff to make you smack yo' lips."

Rocking back and forth several times before she could get up from the sofa, her joints had become stiff from sitting so long. Finally erecting her stance, she stood with grace and refused my help.

"Gal ain't got it like she used to and I wish I didn't have it when I met Rufus, that ol' man I married." She continued to talk as she lumbered her Amazon body toward the kitchen.

"Well chile 'bouts yo' Aunt Lucille. Lucille loved herself sum Lucille. And men loved her more than that. Hell, I loved her." Realizing what she had said, she hurriedly set things straight, "In a normal human being kinda love. I ain't one of them fruit cups."

I had never heard anyone say fruit cups before, but each person has his own descriptions. Assuming she was talking about homosexuals, I dared not question that any further.

She came back with the lemonade and gave me a glass. Then she sat back down on the sofa. Taking a sip from her glass, she continued her story.

"I 'member Lucille took me up to this big house wit' her. I don't know whose house it b'longs to but Lucille knew and everybody calling her out by name and speaking to her, no one knows I was there. I members the room was very large, filled wit' smoke and whiskey drankin'. We walked past this huge green table top they called a pool table, stained wit' old water rings on the wood from one corner of the table to the other. The table had a bunch o' men standing 'round it and some propped up on stools holding them sticks.

Women wuz buzzing 'round like it was summertime and all this while Bobby Blue Bland record was playing. I still 'member the words to that song 'cause I bought it and played it to death." She began to sing the song with a trembling voice, "♫ You know my room caught on fire, you told my landlord to turn on the heat, oh yes you did . . . I was down in my bed with pneumonia girl, and you sprinkled ice cubes all around my feet, oh yeah . . . oh, if you got a heart girl, oh it must be made out of ice♫"

"Bobby sang that song chile. The deeper you walked in that smoke filled house, the less I could hear Bobby tell that not so sweet story 'bout a country gurl on his record. Some of the folks, as we pass through, wuz playing cards and slammin' them cards down hard each time and talking trash. Utha folks was dancin', drankin', eatin' and doin' what we called back then as shootin' the jive. Everybody was having a good time." Once again Aunt Charity released a chuckle.

I assumed all this talk released a floodgate of memories. I smiled with appreciation, listening as she eagerly shared.

Then Aunt Charity said, "You know chile, sumbody musta love that song by Bobby Blue Bland, mo' than me, 'cause they turned it up loud. 'cause I hears his voice in the back of the house wit'out strain. And Bobby continued to sang his song and I kep' on sangin' wit' him, ♫ I work so hard for you baby b'ought you every dime, oh yes, and I ax ya what mo' can I do, you said go out and catch a lil overtime and my mama call you lil daughter do wrong, mama knows you will neva be nice, she says, son, if that gurl's got a heart don't you know it's got to be made of ice♫.

By the time Bobby had reached these words my eyes was closed, I was swaying and snapping my fangers to the beat. When that song stopped playing, I opened my eyes long e'nuff to catch a glimpse of Lucille finishing up a slow dance wit' a good looking mane. And chile before they stopped moving them feet, they was going up them stairs. At that time, I didn't know that this house was where mos married men met them other women."

"Another woman that's not their wife?" I said, sounding and acting dumb as I posed my question.

"Yeah, ain't that nuttin'? But it would take God to tell me Lucille didn't know."

"Yes, that is something Aunt Charity," I said, patronizing her.

"Yeah and you know sumttin' chile."

"No, but I will after you tell me." I suddenly realized that that comment could have sounded like a smart mouth. Evidently she didn't because she kept talking.

"I met the man I married there."

"You did? Was he married when you met him and did you know he would be your husband and did you meet him that night?"

"Hell naw, he wasn't married. And I knew he could be my husband just as any mane could be one day. I met his sorry ass anutha night when I went again wit' Lucille to that big ol' house."

"I didn't mean to insult you Aunt Charity, but when you said married men met women there . . ."

"I said, 'most men', not all, quote right."

"I'm sorry."

"My husband was too." Then she began to yawn.

"Are you tired?"

"Naw chile, I's enjoying the comp'ny."

"Me too," I suggested.

Time was flying by and I needed to get home.

"Aunt Charity," I said as I also began to yawn.

"Yes." She said.

"What happened to Aunt Lucille?"

"While sittin there watching the steps waiting for her to come down, there was a good looking mane sittin next to me keeping me comp'ny and I's glad he did, cause it was getting late and I was sleepy; finally she came down. Them folks in there might thought I was a fruit cup, excited as I got when I saw her. I was acting like them men folk act. She went up dressed in a black A-line dress wit a matching jacket but she came back down in a long black mink coat. She musta talked some deal up wit that mane. I guess she still had on the dress and the jacket. All I know is she still had on her shoes, that's all I could see."

"Where did she get the coat from?"

"Chile, I guess you need help on everythang. From one of the many men that loved her."

"Was it real?"

"Sho' it was, Lucille didn't fool wit' nuttin not real, 'cluding people. People called her a ho', but I say she was a good ho'."

"Aunt Lucille was quite an interesting person."

"She sho' was," she repeated herself, "she, sho' was. She had lots of pretty thangs, wanted to give my country ass some. But my body and feet was too big for her lil cute stuff. But you know that fur coat was the death of her."

"How?" I asked.

"You can ax me anything else but I gots to go take a piss." Aunt Charity stated as she got up and went to the restroom.

Much time passed as I sat and sat, drifting off to sleep.

CHAPTER 12

W hen she returned she startled me, clearing her throat as she replied, "I feel much betta now; you can go on wit yo' talk," as she sat down next to me.

Saying to myself, *she must have had to do more than pee.*

Once she sat down, I excused myself and got up to go to the rest room to relieve my bladder hoping this would give her opportunity to reflect, anticipating that I would repeat my last question.

When I returned, before I could sit down, she started talking, I knew she was ready.

She began, "Lucille and Mabel wents to Detroit together, even up there people loved her. Mabel said she couldn't even go to the ball diamond without men fallin all at her feet. And by then Mabel had gotten herself married and had a daughter and a son. Without getting married, Lucille had a daughter, named her Queen.

Queen was about the age twelve and spoiled rotten and Lucille still never wurked a day in her life, but her chile didn't hurt fo' nuttin'. They dressed, lived and ate good. They be kept like queens."

"That surely was a pretty name for her daughter," not realizing I had said that out loud.

"Sho' it was. And a lil queen she was 'til the day her mama died."

"Yes Aunt Charity, how did Aunt Lucille die?"

"To me, it was mo' 'portant how she lived, but I will tell you how she died, if that's the question that's gon' stay on yo' mind."

"Yes, I really would like to know. Its significance carries a great weight."

"Alrhat then, Lucille and I had become good friends. No matters how yo' grandmama treat me, Lucille had a great heart, so did Mabel. But I hated yo' mean ass grandmama, she was straight from hell, without a pitchfork. 'Cuse me for my cussin," she apologized.

"It's okay," I assured her.

"Hell, I didn't pologize for you to forgive me, I 'pologize for my cussin'; only God can forgive me. But I did hate her to the bone, treat me lo'er than a snakes belly, so that tells you how low I was."

I thought to myself, *"Please tell me how did Aunt Lucille die?"*

She must have read my mind and said, "Lucille was great and Mabel treated me good most of the time, but Lucille always the same. When Lucille left for Detroit, I cried for weeks 'cause I miss her and I cain't stay in that house wit Aunt Charity and Uncle Jack, 'specially all the girls gon', I be by myself. I had nobody to hope me. Honey had married Mitch, so I didn't have to worry 'bout her and I married my husband, rest his devil soul." She smiled a wicked smile that could give a body chills.

She continued, "After years in Detroit and she would visit of'en, but one day Lucille came home for her last visit; neither one of us knew that would be the last time that I'd see her alive." Tears streamed down her cheeks, but she carried her words onward, causing her words to be so broken that I could hardly understand them.

Feeling genuine compassion for her pain, all I could do was extend a Kleenex and a shoulder if she needed one. Interrupting her tears and hoping this would be the last time I ask, "Please Aunt Charity, don't get angry at me for asking this question, but I need to know."

"Needs to know or wants to know?" sounding cross.

"Need to know." Saying it as gentle as I possibly could.

"Was Aunt Lucille, before she died, considered a whore?"

The reaction she displayed came upon me with a surprise. Laughing out loud she caused me to flinch. The laughter seemed to be the sound of joyful delight.

"Lots of people said she be a ho', but I says she got what she wanted for her and Queen, and mens got what they wanted from her. Seeing it be's an even swap to me. Them men folk were pleased, she was comfortable and her child be happy. If that be's a ho', I shoulda had sense to be one too, but me being a fool, married a mane who gave me nuttin' but heartache and his last name. And that brangs me nuttin' but tears. Now all the tears I got left is for memories of Lucille and my arthritic knees."

"How did she hide all her activities with men, from her child?" I asked.

"No man comes in over her child, 'specially them married ones. If they visit, they come when Queen be gone or she be sleep. But her child comes furst."

"I can respect that." I responded.

"No matter if you respect it or don't respect it, it don't matter wit Lucille whether she be 'live or she be dead."

Aunt Charity seemed to protect Aunt Lucille even with the knowledge of her being gone forever. I decided not to apologize for the flow of my insulting words, afraid that if I did my head would be placed in the lion's mouth. I realized how much she loved Aunt Lucille and I realized she was tolerating me.

"After Lucille passed, Aunt Charity keeps Queen and raise her, since Uncle Jack's stayings away came mo' often than his beings home, Aunt Charity had nobody in that big ol' house wit her. Loneliness purt'ner drove her crazy. Mabel be's livin' in Detroit, Uncle Jack gone, Lucille dead, Honey Mae's be in her own selfish world, nobody left but Queen."

"Grandma Charity raised Queen huh?"

"Till she died. We's don't know what killed her. She jus' got sick one day and the doctor did all he could to get her well. Doc Bug loved that family and they money too."

I remember my grandmother telling me how devastated she was when her mother passed away because not only did she lose her mother, but she had lost her best friend, maybe her only friend in the world.

"Well Aunt Charity, what happened to Queen?"

"Po' Queen hads to live wit' yo' bitch grandmama Honey Mae. Felt sorry fo' the child 'cause Honey Mae really didn't want her, but Mabel last born child, Carnell, came out a retard. Mabel's hands was full wit' him, put all her heart into his livin'. Didn't hear much from Mabel, 'cept on Christmas and funerals. I guess you thank with all the dying we had, we saw her often?" She laughed, "Chile, you asked me what happened to Lucille didn't you?'

"Finally!" I said to myself, but I dared not ask again.

"Well Lucille won't much on takin' care o' hurself, not like she was at taking care of Queen. Wish she had been, she might still be in the land of the livin'. One night though, Lucille drop Queen off over Mabel's to stay the night so she's could go out and fetch herself a good time at the juke joint wit' grown folks. They tells me it was the coldest night in Detroit and the snow wuz up to yo' thigh, but you know that ain't nuttin' for them up north, but us down here in the south, we stop movin' 'round wit' one flake.

Anyhow's, Lucille went out in that snow dressed all pretty and she had that long black mink on. Gots down at the juke joint, smokin', drankin and cussin' and gots mad at the man who owns the place cause he didn't want to give her no mo' whiskey. He wanted her to go lay down in the back and sleep some of that ol' liquor off, fo' she try to go home, but she git wild and was fit to be tied. He didn't give up, he wo'e her down tusslin' till she passed out in his arms. Den he put her in bed and went back to sell his whiskey and makes him some mo' money. He knowed won't nobody hurt Lucille cause everybody know he takes good care of her and she might later on, takes good care of him.

Early that next mornin' when he closed up his juke joint, he goes in back to check on her, but when he got there, she be gon'."

"Where was she?" I quickly jumped in with great excitement.

"Hold yo' ho'ses chile, I's gon' tell ya'." She chuckled at my anticipation, and said, "Gon' home and when I says gon' home I means gon' home.

They found Lucille how she be headed home. She slipped out the back do' of the juke joint. It had snowed sum mo'. She had took off wit'out puttin' on that mink coat. She was walking home in the snow almost naked. Home was 'bout a mile from the juke joint. And she ain't had nuttin' on! By's the time they found her, she was dead as a do'knob."

I could see the pain written all over Aunt Charity's face.

"She died on me, my good friend died on me. We be's young . . ." Shaking her head gently back and forth, "we thought we lives forever. She was only 24 years old when she leave here, but now she got her place in heaven. I'll bet all the angels lovin' her and always hangin' 'round her, just like we did here on earth."

Grieving, suddenly Aunt Charity slapped her knees really hard and said, "Well I guess it's time fo' you to be leavin' me now huh?"

I didn't know whether to feel insulted; I didn't know whether I was being put out or, in her own special way, kindly asking me to leave.

Then she said, "I's tired and I know you's tired too and ready to go."

Hesitantly I said, stammering, "Yeh . . . yeh . . . yes, it really is late and I do have to drive across town," convincing myself that my leaving was partly my idea. While putting my coat on, Aunt Charity assisted me with my purse.

"Now you listen chile, you come back to see an old lady sum," as she was walking me to the door.

"I will and I enjoyed myself and it was good to meet you." Giving her a hug, I said, "I will come to see you again, I promise."

She patted me on the back as I went out the door. Once I got inside my car, I looked back, and there she was still standing and watching. I thought; *"she's probably making sure I got in safe."* After starting the car, I put it in drive, paused for a moment, turned and grabbed another look at her. Then I waved and pulled off. Driving along slowly I could still hear her chuckle in my ears and it made me smile.

The next day I called Aunt Charity concerning a question I had forgotten to ask her the night before. Unfortunately, calling her was easy, getting off the phone wasn't. However, I did get to ask my question.

"Aunt Charity, you mentioned you had two sons, where are they?"

"One's in Heaven, 'longside they's grandma and grandpa. The other one's near me, God left him to give me the hope I need as an old woman."

I wanted to ask her why she didn't say her dead son was with his father, but opted to let sleeping dogs lie as I hung up the telephone.

CHAPTER 13

The next morning while drinking a cup of coffee and recanting my pleasant night with Aunt Charity, I began to remember the story of when my grandmother told me . . .

Months had gone by and she still had not seen Mitch, she had come to the realization, he was gone out of her life forever, blaming no one but herself.

Since Charity had come to live with them, my grandmother decided she did not want to live in the house with country trash. She had decided to make Charity's life as miserable as hers. She felt above sharing her quarters with a cousin maid. She considered herself too sassy and sophisticated to be associated with Charity.

Avoiding her cousin as much as possible, she found herself leaving home much earlier each morning headed for school. School was nearing its year's end and none too soon for Honey Mae, especially since she was keeping a promise she had made to an unknowing Mitch, making education a priority.

However, the invitation for summer recess was a truly welcomed one. Everyone was excited about the change of season. The weather was warm, the leaves had turned green, the grass was growing and the sky was embellished with white fluffy clouds. Humming birds were flying around their nests investigating for any need of reconstruction. Days were absolutely beautiful. God couldn't have made anything better than the creation of nature.

On this particular day, Honey Mae decided on her early morning venture to school to go past her house that once was a home for her and her Aunt Callie and Uncle Fodie. When she arrived, she noticed the old trash wagon piled high with rubble from the property, but there was no driver.

She knew it had to be Mitch; he was the only owner of the town's trash wagon. Her heart began to rush. Each pounding beat seemed to overpower her ears as she thought, *"Please God let it be him."* From her lips the prayer must have fallen on God's ears because before she could finish asking God, Mitch came from alongside the house.

Hoisted on his shoulder, he was carrying a large stack of burned timber. Working without paying attention, he finally looked up and saw Honey Mae standing there. He said nothing, just continued his work.

Thinking long and careful before she opened her mouth, afraid of what may come out and believing this may be her last chance to save what she thought could be the man that would be with her for the rest of her life, she thought before speaking.

"What should I say Lord?" Surprisingly she prayed. *"Should I stay, should I walk away? Would he want to hear anything I have to say?"*

While she thought, Mitch never acknowledged her presence, not even to say good morning. However, each time he came from around the house, his load looked smaller, signaling he was almost finished with his work. She was running out of time. The very last time he came to the front, he only had a couple of pieces in his hand.

He threw them onto his wagon and began to mount when all of a sudden he felt a tug at his overalls, he turned and looked around. Not giving her a chance to speak, he asked professionally, "How may I help you ma'am?"

"Ma'am?" She questioned, not so politely.

Looking at her for a few seconds, he turned away and continued mounting onto his wagon.

"Damn," she said softly, almost in a whisper. Swallowing her pride, she touched him on his back.

"Wait, Mitch, please," she said, her words quite sincere.

He climbed down from the wagon, turning, looking in her face once again. She hurriedly noticed there was no gleam that danced in his eyes when he looked at her.

"Wait for what!" he said almost angrily, "you told me what to do and where to go, so sweet lady, I'm on my way and as a matter of fact, consider me already there."

Hurt and annoyed, he didn't stop there, "I've lost an important part of my life, my father, so losing what I didn't have with you, grieves me none. So little lady, if that's all . . . I need to move on, I have work to do."

"But there is something else," she said, "I need to ask you. Why are you here? Why are you picking trash up from this property?" She was concerned about their relationship, but she was also concerned of why he was at her house.

"Ain't really your business, but I'll answer your question. I was hired to clean off this land and haul the rubble away."

"Hired by whom?"

"You sure are the nosy one?"

"Humor me, please."

He was smiling inside because he could get use to her saying please to him; it was much nicer to his ears than her ranting and cursing, which she was so free to give. "You wouldn't know them."

"Try me."

"Well if you have to know and be pushy, Mr. and Mrs. Watkin Jackson. Maybe you would know them; you have the same last name."

"That's because, they're my mother and father."

His face showed surprise, "No kidding?"

"Trust me, I wish I was, at least about my father, we don't always see eye to eye."

"Oh really?" He spoke sarcastically.

"Let's just say we had a few pitfalls."

"A pitfall with you lady, can lead a man straight to hell. You can make him or shatter him, interest him or disinterest him." He spoke adamantly.

"I hope you stay interested, and I'm sorry what happened to your father. I didn't know about his death. However, it doesn't excuse my not being considerate because I was hurting also. You see, this old burned down house is where my Aunt and Uncle lost their lives and it's where I was living at the time. When it happened, I was in school. When they died, they left me this property."

"That was you, they've been talking about around town? That everyone was feeling sorry for?" By this time his sympathy had grown.

"People were feeling sorry for me?" She paused for a brief moment, "Well, yes, that was me they were talking about."

Pulling off his work gloves, leaning against his wagon, he began to listen and she began to talk. On that day, Honey Mae didn't make it to school. She stayed helping Mitch and they never stopped talking. Not only did she get dirty, she also received many hugs and kisses beyond her imagination. For days, they met at the same place, around the same time, falling in love with each other.

Charity knew her child was happy again, and when she learned the happiness was brought by the young man named Mitch Purify, she was elated.

Mitch shared with Honey all the time he could, even if it meant having to work longer hours in order to make up for lost time from his business, anything to help them find each other. But no matter how much time he gave, inside, she wanted more.

Vowing never to let this emotion rear its ugly head, she accepted what he could give. The summer days seemed to evaporate quicker than dew under a hot August sun. Hot were the days, but not as heated as the romance of Honey and Mitch. Their love excelled. Their days were not long enough and the nights were too long, separating their kisses and embraces. Their passion grew strong and they became disappointed when time wouldn't stand still because they knew soon summer vacation would be over and the school days were about to begin.

The first day of school came bright and early. Mitch rode up to the front of the house and everyone excitedly ran out and loaded onto the wagon as he drove them all to school. Lucille, Mabel, Willie, Hannah and Charity all piled into the back of the wagon and Honey Mae haughtily sat up front with Mitch.

After arriving at their destination, they all unloaded and started up the hill when they turned and saw Honey Mae still planted next to Mitch, hugging and kissing. They all began to giggle. After the school bell had rang, Honey Mae finally entered the classroom and sat down at her desk. The teacher, Ms. Gibbs, just shook her head and said nothing.

Sitting in the midst of class, Honey Mae thought she should have stayed at home. She couldn't think or hear anything; her mind was on Mitch and time passed slowly. Twirling her fingers in her hair, she doodled on her paper. Suddenly, in the distance she heard a faint but very familiar, distinct sound that peeked her attention. The sound drew nearer and she grew anxious.

Ms. Gibbs, looked up from grading papers after she heard the sound of a desk moving against the floor. Not surprised to find it was Honey Mae's desk, Ms. Gibbs stared into her eyes. Honey swiftly returned her eyes back down to her papers, pretending to do her class work.

The sound of the horse hooves was close to the school yard. Looking out the window, she could feel her heart racing and her palms sweating. Soon she saw the wagon peak over the top of the hill. She began twisting and turning in her seat causing the chair to make the loud scraping sound on the floor. Once again, Ms. Gibbs' attention was placed upon her.

"Miss Jackson," She yelled.

The other students, busy with their quiz, were startled looking up at the same time, including Mabel and Lucille. She left them wondering which Miss Jackson she was referring to. However, Honey Mae already knew.

Ms. Gibbs repeated her command, "Miss Jackson!"

Honey Mae gave her words no thought. Ms. Gibbs saw that she did not have Honey Mae's attention, so she yelled even louder while slapping her yard stick down on her desk. "Miss Jackson, I'm speaking to you!"

At this point Lucille and Mabel knew Ms. Gibbs was not speaking to the two of them. Mabel released a sigh of relief, "Whew," while at the same time wiping her forehead. Lucille said in a low muddled tone, "Ahh hell, here comes trouble."

By this time the entire class was no longer focused on their test papers. They were focused on the test of wills between Honey Mae and Ms. Gibbs—wills they had all seen before.

Without thinking Lucille blurted out, "My money is on my sister."

Everyone laughed; this angered their teacher. Annoyed with the unruly behavior exhibited by the sassy young lady, she called out her name once more, "Miss Jackson."

This time Honey Mae looked in her direction.

"Now do I have your attention?"

Honey Mae gave a quick smirk. Accepting this, Ms. Gibbs said, "Good, let's get back to our class work."

Everyone seemed to abide by their teacher's request, all except one.

She began unlacing her ankle high boots, taking them off and placing them neatly on the floor side by side. Charity could see her actions from her peripheral view, but did not inquire. However, Lucille began to question, herself thinking, *"What is she up to now?"*

Honey now dressed in her whiter than white stocking feet, closed her book, placed her pencil down on the desk and walked toward the open window. Propping one foot on the sill while the other balanced her on the floor, the entire class began to snicker, including Charity.

Slowly learning she was losing control of the class, when Ms. Gibbs looked up her attention was focused on Honey Mae perched on the window like a pigeon. Before she could finish calling out the name, "Honey Mae Jackson," she had thrown her shoes to the ground hoisted her legs out the window followed by a jump to the ground.

Falling to her hands and knees, she tore her stockings, noticing blood stains on one leg. She got up and dusted herself off. Taking a quick glance back at her escape hatch, she found all her classmates standing in the window, screaming with excitement. She laughed out loud as they were cheering her on.

Lucille, most visible to her, gave her thumbs of approval, while Mabel was crying like a frightened baby. Ms Gibbs, pushing her way through the thickness of her students, finally, made her way over and yelled, "Young lady, I'm going to have a talk with your parents!" Even in anger placing her words in perfect order, "Come back to this classroom this instant!"

The threat of her parents fueled Honey Mae causing her to be even more disrespectful. Divorcing herself from the school ordinance she turned and looked in her teacher's face screaming, "I don't give a good got damn, what you tell those bitches! While you're at it stick them up your ass! And as for coming to your classroom," she gave a curtsy and said, "I bow the hell out."

Then she turned her back to the school, bent over and smacked both sides of her butt and said, "Especially tell my daddy, to take the nearest exit to hell and kiss me in the center of my ass on the way out."

She then shook her butt cheeks with her hands, turned her head, looking over her shoulder stuck out her tongue before she ran up the hill.

From among the crowd, someone released a loud whistle. Ms. Gibbs stood there and said in a low tone, "How unlady like."

Running up the hill, she could still hear the loud whistles, claps and cheers that she was leaving behind. She didn't give another thought as to whether Ms. Gibbs approved or disapproved or whether she regained order in the classroom that was now the teacher's problem.

Finally reaching where the wagon and Mitch stood, she leaped into his waiting arms. Even though he found her behavior outrageous and ridiculous, he somehow found it appealing that she would go through so much trouble to be with him. It heightened his suspicions of her mental instability, but filled him with momentum and intrigue that captured him in a world of amazement and accentuated his swelling desire like a hemotoma.

Then he began questioning himself with questions he already knew the answers to. *"What have I gotten myself into? What have I fallen in love with?"*

Finally out loud he asked, "Why did you jump out of that window?'

She answered, "I had a window of opportunity to graduate early and I jumped to it."

"Graduated early." He said.

Trying to be coy and cute but yet deceptive she replied, "All the applause you hear from the class in the background, is attributed to me, because I graduated with honors."

Mitch smiled, at her recklessness and her wickedness. But he questioned her no further, forgetting about his philosophy for education and she forgot her unspoken promise.

Leaping into his arms, she lay against his chest and her toes elevated from the ground. She placed her hands on his flexed biceps as they danced the same rhythm as the first day she laid eyes on his massive structure. Holding her close, she took in a deep breath, gathering the fragrance of his cleanliness. Closing her eyes, she awaited his kiss. Instead he gently blew his breath across her face, leaving her wanting the feel of his moist lips.

With his hands firmly around her, he began to glide her down, lowering her to the ground, her breast caressed his large chest walls, allowing her sense of feel against her thighs to obtain knowledge of the aroused sensation that was bursting through his body with a sense of urgency.

Almost unaware of her feet touching the ground, Mitch leaned down and gave her a passionate and feverish kiss, a kiss they both had yearned for. After a long minute of strong heated temperatures, Mitch picked Honey Mae up once again, placing her on the wagon. Without notice, another cheer came from the background. When they looked around, the schoolyard was filled with students and much enthusiasm, including their teacher Ms. Gibbs, with her arms folded in front of her, watching as they drove away.

One week later, they were married.

CHAPTER 14

Moving into the house with Mitch and his siblings made adjustments somewhat difficult. However, adjusting to them was no problem as long as things went Honey Mae's way. And her way they went.

Mitch had the muscles, but now Honey Mae flexed hers. Willie and Hannah hated her from the start and veered out of her way as much as possible. Honey was wicked.

The downhill of Honey Mae and Mitch's relationship almost began on their honeymoon because he had lost control of his family. However, he didn't see or realize it until much later. Hannah often told him to take his blinders off, Willie never said a thing, but it was very noticeable that he agreed with Hannah.

Mitch summed their actions and words as jealousy because now he had to share his attention with them and his new bride. They knew they had lost their brother the first night Honey Mae became Mrs. Mitchell Purify, and what a night of wedding bliss it was.

All had been preplanned by her and every detail had been well executed. So detailed, she had even calculated how many times she would stroke his head. Love was one thing, but losing power to it was another. She had to keep complete control especially over Mitch.

Lying in bed waiting for his bride, a minute seemed like an hour. He grew with impatience and anticipation, so he called out to her, "Where is my sweet lady?"

No answer, he called again. Still no answer.

He feared something had happened. Had she possibly fainted? As he started to get out of bed, she heard his movement on the bedspring; she realized he may be coming for her. So quickly, she turned the doorknob leading to their bedroom and he got back in bed.

Opening the door, she entered. He expected her to be dressed in a long high-neck cotton gown, but instead to his astonishment, she had on a sheer, long, black robe with nothing underneath. The light shining from the next room outlined her silhouette as she stood with her legs apart.

Mitch was covered by a white sheet draped over his lower body, but allowing one of his well glazed gladiator legs to be exposed. Walking slowly across the room, she revealed her long infinite silky shapely body for the first time to her husband.

Lifting one leg on a footstool, she placed it strategically, just out of Mitch's reaching distance. Her schemes had begun; her web was stretched out wide.

Seductively dancing her fingers slowly up her leg then pushing the sheerness of the nylon covering past her upper thigh, she gave a glimpse of her treasure of pleasure.

She could see his acceptance beneath the sheet as he lay stretched out on the bed. Quickly noting the sight that was frightfully large, she became apprehensive but told herself it was nothing she couldn't handle.

He started to speak, but she walked closer to the bedside and placed her index finger against his lips indicating not to say a word. He then reached out and tried to touch her long exotic leg which seemed to call his name but she stopped his advances.

At this point, seeing what could possibly be the imprint of his large sexual organ, she questioned herself, *"Am I still seducing him or am I stalling?"*

Stepping back, she turned to go and put a record on the phonograph. Then she began swerving her hips and spinning around creating a seductive dance to the music. He was salivating. Gracefully gliding back over to the reach of Mitch, she did not remove his hands once he began to touch her. This time she assisted him. Easing his fingertips on her thigh, she caused him to close his eyes, slowly creeping and moving his hands toward the glorious moment he longed for since the day they met.

While he was touching her, she leaned forward to allow him full view and the taste of sweetness from her swollen breast. Overheated, Mitch pulled her over his body onto the bed, kissing her breast even more. He began kissing her all over, vigorously making love to his wife, but oh so gentle. She made him groan with great pleasure. They made love until they were both exhausted, falling asleep in each others arms.

Awake before Honey, he sat in the chair across the room, watching his new bride sleep in angelic peace. Like a warm blanket, his every thought was of her touch, of her fragrance, her kiss, her love making and being with him forever.

Her plan had worked; he had been captured in the web of a spider.

He, basking in his heaven on earth, smiled for indeed his wife had served him well, being a virgin she left him quite happy.

After a wonderful night she finally woke after hearing the record which they had played the night before scraping its edge against the phonograph's needle. Mitch had been playing the songs again.

Opening her eyes slightly, she smiled when she saw her husband's face across the room. He was sitting in the chair, staring lovingly at his wife. He got back in bed making love to his wife over and over and over again.

When the new days began, routine in the Purify house were not so routine any longer. Routine could not live in the same home with Honey Mae. She had Willie and Hannah doing things Mitch wouldn't have them to do before. She took them away from their studies. They had taken the place of Charity, they had become her maid.

She would make them serve her coffee at the table while she sat there with her legs crossed; she made them clean house and no matter how well the work was done, she found complaints.

Telling Mitch did no good. In his eyes, his wife did no wrong besides Honey was great at throwing rocks and hiding her hands. She transformed situations to make herself look the martyr.

Hannah and Willie learned to walk on eggshells. Willie was able to ignore her, but Hannah was frightened to death. Once Honey beat Hannah so bad when they were alone, her back was discolored for weeks. Honey made her keep it a secret, threatening to make it worse the next time if she said anything to her brothers.

She remained submissive to Honey's rules, telling only her husband O.Z. after they were married. Then she made him promise never to tell, which he reluctantly agreed. They were married before Hannah could finish school, going against Mitch and her parents wishes, but she had to get out of that house.

O.Z. loved Hannah but three years after their marriage, she became suddenly ill and died a short time later, bringing great devastation. By the time they buried Hannah, O.Z. made known the cruelty that Hannah suffered at the hands of Mitch's wife.

No longer surprised with information of his wife's evil capabilities, he knew the honeymoon was over. However, the love making was still great—great enough to create two sons, Mitch Jr. and Bobby.

Hannah died, never getting to know her nephews. Broken hearted was Mitch because he no longer had a close relationship with his sister or brother since they had left home. He only connected with his sister the last few weeks of her life.

By now Mitch no longer had his trash wagon; times had changed. He now worked for the United States Steel (TCI). Mitch took time from work along with Willie, now married to Tomorrow, often to help O.Z. care for their ailing beloved sister.

Once, out of frustration, O.Z. lashed out at Mitch blaming Mitch for allowing Honey to create Hannah's illness, which was a broken heart. Mitch lowered his head in shame.

O.Z.'s voice became louder, "Look at you man, a coward. You need to go and see if God will let you purchase a new spine because the one you had was donated to Honey Mae." Then O.Z. broke down and cried, falling into Mitch's arms.

Mitch held him tight whispering, "I'm sorry."

O.Z. wept more. Once he gathered his composure, he pulled away and apologized to his brother-in-law, whom he had grown to love and said, "I'm sorry too, I didn't mean what I said, I'm just hurting." His voice cracked as his tears continued to flow.

"I know man, I know, I'm hurting also."

For about an hour they sat at the dining room table with nothing else said between them but they had the security of knowing the other was there. Then O.Z. went back in to sit with Hannah. Mitch followed a few minutes later.

A few days later Hannah passed in her husband's arms giving him his last kiss before saying, "Goodbye."

Honey decided not to attend the funeral with Mitch, telling him that the babies were too young and there was no one she wanted to leave them with.

Knowing this was an excuse or just another way to disrespect his sister even in death, he walked away. His 'blinders', as Hannah would often call them, had been removed. He began noticing; not even death could strip away Honey's selfish, wicked ways. Her only desire in life was to raise hell.

After the funeral, everyone gathered at the home of O.Z. and Hannah. The guests stayed into the late hours of the night. Everyone was celebrating the memory of Hannah with drinks, much food and good conversation; she would have been pleased with her homegoing.

However, before his sister's death, Mitch had already begun drinking heavily, something he had never done before.

Seeing his brother have drink after drink drew concern for Willie. He monitored him during the gathering and making sure he was alright. But a short while later when he was not watching, Mitch had disappeared. Frantically looking for him in the crowd, frustrated and not wanting to alarm anyone of his concern, he started to believe his brother had possibly walked home drunk. He was right.

Mitch arrived home safe but did not go inside; instead he slept in the new car he had bought previously. Filled with betrayal of his trust, he eventually started staying away from home more and drinking Joe Louis whiskey just as much.

Provisions for home had become rare and bare causing Honey Mae's anger to grow. Never having worked before, she began looking and asking for domestic work—something she had become quite acquainted with and was good at since there was no more maid service. By now the money she received from Fodie and Callie was long gone.

Spending frivolously, buying items such as jewelry, furs, shoes, clothes, she bought everything that was expensive. When their mother Charity died the girls received no money because all funds were still tied to their father.

He would help Mabel and Lucille whenever needed, but his relationship with Honey was never mended. Jack made several attempts, but they died each time he requested her presence. Even at the graveside of Charity, she stayed her distance from him. She stood there emotionally distraught, hand in hand with Mitch and as usual, he stood tall and handsome.

Mitch adored his wife as she wore a black fur hat that seemed to cascade down to a matching, floor sweeping mink coat. Capturing the eyes of all entering into her presence, she relished every moment.

Her outward appearance wasn't real or true, but her outcry for her dead mother was all too genuine. Even Charity felt compassion for her sorrow. Jack walked over to help Mitch console his daughter, but was quickly rejected.

On that day she declared to her father, making it plain and clear, "Consider yourself dead and I'm burying you along with Charity."

CHAPTER 15

Life in the Purify household had become unbearable. In the beginning of their relationship was where neither could get enough of the other. Mitch would leave for work every morning after having coffee and breakfast with his wife; she mostly had coffee and a cigarette, a habit that had quickly become her second love. Breakfast was always guaranteed to be served with an extra helping of love making. 24 hours was not enough time in a day for their love.

Recently Mitch had bought one of the camp housing, that the steel mill had built for their employees in the Negro community, Honey was happy with their new home. Mitch sold their old house and split the proceeds between himself and Willie.

Their new home, being on the campus of the steel mill, made it easy for Mitch to come home often for lunch. Coming home for lunch for the first few years of their marriage was a treat, but soon the only time he came home from work was to kiss his children or sleep off a drunk.

Lovemaking for the two of them had stopped a long time ago; now they just had explosive sex. Time had begun to take its toll on the lifeless marriage. One morning after Mitch had left for work, Honey Mae gathered the boys for a trip to the commissary for a new pair of shoes and pants. The ones they owed were worn and torn.

Arriving at the commissary, she was dressed in a brown, tweed suit, the scarf-like collar of the jacket swept its way across her chest from one shoulder to the other while the back of the collar stood touching the nape of her neck, reflecting elegance and style. The pencil thin skirt stopped two inches below the knee causing her stride to be cut short. Her attire was complimented with brown leather three-inch stilettos, matching handbag and gloves.

Bobby and Mitch Jr. were well groomed and dressed in creased navy pants starched white shirts and glowing high top, hard bottom laced shoes. Each had a matching brown coat and cap. What a family picture this displayed.

When Honey Mae came into the room, she spoke out loud, "Hello everyone."

Receiving only a few responses, she didn't care. Whispers started to flow around the room; this made Honey Mae smile, for this was the kind of attention she thrived on. People discussing her, whether good or bad, added fuel to her ability to increase people's hatred toward her.

Her logic behind this was if they are talking about her, they must be thinking about her. Gracefully she walked up to the store counter, almost gliding like she was on a sheet of ice. Like a figure skater, her head held high and like a model, she owned the runway. Little did she know, lying ahead was a head on collision.

The store owner respected Honey Mae and her fierce ways, but he was even more afraid to cross Mitch and his orders as a US Steel worker. Mitch was one of his most reliable customers. Most of the time he paid cash for his purchases, but sometimes he used an open account for the convenience of his family, never failing to pay his bill on time.

The store owner knew Honey didn't work and, no matter what, he knew who really owned the account.

"Good Morning." She said directly to the girl working behind the counter.

"Good Morning Honey Mae," the clerk responded, "how may I help you?'

The clerk's demeanor was unusual; she was acting nervous. Honey Mae noticed, but never asked what was wrong.

"I came in this morning to get my boys some shoes, pants and shirts. They need them; they seem to grow overnight. I also have a list of groceries I'll be needing, I have everything written down," she said as she extended the paper over to the young lady.

She took it from Honey, walked over and gave it to Mr. Cummins. Honey found this strange because the clerk always filled her orders and never once had she given it to Mr. Cummins. With hesitance, he came over to speak to her. She was smiling as he approached.

Clearing his throat, "I'm sorry, but you can't get anything on this account."

Filled with surprise, the pleasant voice disappeared and she said, "What the hell do you mean I can't get anything on this account?" The smile left her face and her words became loud. Everyone stopped their business in the store to tend to hers.

Proudly she said, "I know my husband paid this bill."

Standing there in his overall type apron, Mr. Cummins, being a humble man said, "Yes ma'am, he sure did, but he also made some changes."

"What kind of got damn changes?" Her tone unkind.

"He came in and took your name off the account."

"Took my name off the account?" repeating Cummins' words.

One more time he answered with hesitance. "Yes ma'am, he sure did."

"What does taking my name off mean?"

"It means you can't get anything in the commissary unless you pay with your money, but you can't get anything else that Mr. Purify has to buy and pay for later."

If her demeanor and body language were animation; people could see the steam flowing densely from her nostrils and ears. She struggled, trying to remain calm and collected. Honey cupped her son's hands into hers, turned and walked out of the store without further words or incident.

Chills and the hair on the back of Mr. Cummins neck ran deep. She walked a mile in her three inch stilettos never once did she hobble or limp. However, on a couple of occasions she had to scoop Bobby into her arms because he was walking too slow while Jr. trotted alongside them never complaining.

Finally reaching her destination, her father's house, she knew he was not home. She knew he was working. Jack's new wife, Daisy was sitting on the porch wrapped in a blanket, fully dressed underneath, always saying, "no matter the weather, one should always get fresh air daily".

But when Honey Mae saw her, she thought, *"What a got damn weird ass thing to do. If you're cold, take your stupid ass in the house."* She evacuated that thought from her brain because she had bigger fish to fry. Besides she liked Daisy, weird or not, they had gotten along from day one. Partly because Daisy always listened. If her opinion differed from Honey Mae's, she never voiced it. Best of all she loved the boys and treated them like they were her blood grandchildren. They returned to her the same amount of love.

"Hi Daisy, how are you doing?" She asked once on the porch.

Never allowing Daisy to answer her question, she kept her words flowing, "Would you watch my boys for a little while? Thank you, I won't be long. First I need to get something out of the house."

Honey placed Bobby on Daisy's lap and Jr.'s hand on top of Daisy's. She walked into the house straight into her father's den and returned a short while later. Kissed the boys on the forehead, patted Daisy on the shoulder and strutted off the porch onto the yard then onto the street. Keeping a limited stride that the pencil skirt would allow combined with the high heeled shoes, she moved swiftly.

Daisy watched the peacock with her feathers spread wide, stroll out of sight, then gave a laugh and said, "Come on boys, let's go inside and get something to eat, it's cold out here."

Happily they went indoors.

About three hours later, Honey returned, swinging the door wide open. Daisy looked up from the inside marble game she had created on the floor as she played with Bobby and Jr. Causing Honey's response, "What the . . . , never mind, I don't want to know," cutting her words off, Honey dismissed the display of childish behavior on Daisy's behalf and left them with their entertainment.

Uninterrupted, the boys never stopped playing.

"Know what?" Daisy asked.

"What you all are doing?"

"Playing marbles."

"Inside?"

"Inside or out it's still the same game."

Shaking her head Honey sat down, kicked off her shoes, propped her feet on the coffee table and said, "Never mind because I really don't care."

"Good, now do you want something to eat?"

"I'm too mad to eat, but I'll have a drink."

"Smell like you already had one or two, so get up and get you one more."

"Damn you Daisy," Honey said.

"Same to you, but still get up and get your drink," Daisy nonchalantly stated.

Honey got up from the sofa, went into the kitchen and clanged a few glasses around then emerged from the kitchen with a shot glass of liquor. Before she could get to her seat, she had gulped down the alcohol, so she turned around went back into the kitchen and refilled her glass.

By the time she came back to the living room, she had chugged down two shots. Finishing the last one slowly, she joined Daisy watching the boys shoot marbles from one side of the rug to the other.

Suddenly, Honey abruptly said, "Well I guess we'll be going now."

The boys yelled simultaneously, "No!"

Looking at them with an eyebrow arched, pointing her finger at them, "Get up, let's go and not another word." Anger was the sound that erupted from her voice.

Bobby and Jr. jumped to attention, Daisy never said a thing. The boys put on their coats and hats while Honey slipped her feet back into her heels with ease. Leaving out the door with Daisy walking behind them, she lightly tapped Honey on the shoulder causing her to turn and now they were face to face.

Daisy asked, "Did you put it back?"

Looking puzzled, her facial expression gave wonder as to what she was talking about, but her mind knew, so she graciously answered, "Yes, but . . ."

Daisy interrupted, "No buts, you found in this house what you were looking for, then you went into the streets and couldn't find what you were looking for and in the end everything went back to where you started, nowhere. Now go home and fix my grandchildren some dinner," her tone of voice inclining.

If someone else had spoken to Honey in such a manner, even if their words were soft, they would automatically become her mortal enemy. But Daisy was different, so different Honey Mae not only respected her but loved her as well.

"Okay, I'll do that, but I need to make a few stops first; then we'll be headed home." She turned and left, Bobby and Jr. skipping merrily in front of her.

Staggering slightly from the several shots of whiskey, she still walked with grace in her three inch heels. It was an art. On the walk home, Honey Mae began wondering, *"How Daisy knew so much. Maybe she had that thing they called ESP. How in the hell did she know I had taken the gun from my father's den?"*

Almost an hour later, a loud rapping came upon Daisy's front door. Talking to herself she said, *"I know Jack didn't leave his key again."* The knock became louder, Daisy stopped the washing of her dishes, wiped her hands on her apron and yelled, "I'm coming!"

Opening the door only to find Mitch standing there; he wasn't drunk, but she could tell he had had a few. Neatly dressed and smelling good, he always showered before he left work; giving him one less reason to go home.

Giving Daisy a hug he asked, "How's my favorite girl?"

"Your favorite girl is at home with your children, but I'm doing good, thank you."

"Don't start Daisy."

"Don't start what?"

"That family stuff about me, Honey and the children."

"Family stuff is all we got and the two of you have been blessed to add beautiful children to your lives and you too dumb to see past you and Honey. What you two have is something I would have given anything for: children. People that have children take them for granted and people that want to be granted with children can't have them."

This was the first time he had ever heard Daisy imply that she wanted to have children of her own. He knew how much she loved Bobby and Jr. but figured she just decided when she met Jack, she was too old.

Defending himself, "Please Daisy, I know you mean well, but right now I don't want to hear it." He went over to the sofa and dropped down.

"Well don't hear this if you want to, but I'm going to say it. Take your behind over to that commissary and straighten things out for Honey and the boys or you're going to find yourself dead. It's too late for you to tell her what she can and can't have."

His eyes bulged and mouth flung open and heart began to race rapidly. "what do you mean dead?" He asked astounded.

"What, my behind. You heard me loud and clear."

"What is she going to do, kill me?"

"Yes," she said bluntly, "you know not to mess with that girl; she came here to get her father's pistol and that's what she was going to do, kill you, but she couldn't find you. So count your blessings you're still living to set things right. Cause you could be setting it right through your life insurance policy."

Mitch continued sitting on the sofa looking bewildered.

"Now!" Daisy screamed.

He jumped up almost running out the door leaving it wide open.

Daisy said to herself as she was closing the door, *"I'll pray for that crazy couple."*

CHAPTER 16

When Honey Mae and the boys finally arrived home, the temperature had dropped and inside was even colder. Shivering, she made her way over to the gas heater, struck a match, turned the knob releasing gas. Then she placed the match at the opening and the blaze lit up the heater.

The boys loved seeing this sight; however, they never failed to remember their mother's warning and taking heed to never play with matches or around the fire.

By the time she made it to the bedroom to light its heater, she was shocked to behold all the packages on the bed filled with clothes and shoes for the boys and even a dress for her. Attached was a note, 'Sorry for the misunderstanding at the commissary, but you and our children may purchase whatever is needed for home.' She crumbled the note in her hands.

It didn't take long before the heat from the fire and the stove where she had begun dinner, made the house toasty and warm, but not her heart. She still wanted to kill the son of a bitch for her humiliation. Nothing could make up for that.

The house was still; the boys had been fed and given their bath. In the meantime, she was warming a glass of milk for Bobby to drink. This is the only way he would drink milk. Ever since he was an infant, no matter how many times she tried, she couldn't get him to drink cold milk. Also finding it helpful for him to sleep, it was like a soothing sedative.

Jr. had already fallen asleep but Bobby was standing in the kitchen in his footed pajamas, so she picked him up in her arms, swung him around and he giggled with delight.

"Again mommy."

She repeated the act and he repeated his request.

"Again mommy."

"No Bobby, it's time for bed."

"I'm not sleepy."

"Well you are going to bed young man."

"Can I have my milk?"

"Yes, but then it's off to bed."

"Okay." Then he began to yawn.

"I don't think you will make drinking your milk tonight; you'll be sleep before I get it into the glass."

As she was turning off the flame underneath the boiler, she was startled by a hand on her shoulder. She screamed from fear saying, "got damn it!" Turning, she looked into her drunk husband's eyes.

"Hey sweet lady," he stumbled through his words.

Honey gave no response.

Swatting her on the behind, he repeated himself, "Hey sweet lady."

She continued to say nothing, stepping to one side of him, she started to walk away carrying her sleepy child to lay him down. Mitch grabbed her by the other arm, pulling her back against his body. She held tight onto Bobby so she would not drop him.

"Fool! You have lost your damn mind, you are going to make me drop my child."

Still he would not release her, pressing her firmly against his body. She became angry. Once more she tried to move forward trying to walk away. This time he pulled her by her hair.

Trying to sound calm and collected, "Just let me lay our son down."

Taking his tongue and tracing the sweat on her hairline then back down the nape of her neck around to her ear, he whispered, "We'll put our son in bed."

Marching close to her body they went into the children's room and laid him in bed. He was fast asleep.

Trying to free herself from his grip, she was unsuccessful. Pushing her hair away, he began kissing her on the neck again. She just stood there. Using his right hand, his fingers traveled down to the bottom of her pajama top; then he ran his hand underneath it allowing the left hand to join the right as he cupped her breast. He continued to stroke his tongue on the back of her neck while moving his body up and down behind her. He withdrew one hand from underneath her top and explored down to her waist.

Eventually placing his hand inside of her pants, he started to run his hand up and down her thigh. His disregard for her feelings intensified her wrath. But in a warped way, she was trying her best not to be turned on by his behavior while he was in his drunken stupor.

As he moved his hand back and forth on her thigh, he finally found her treasure, the special name he always called her private part. Then he said, "You feel ready for me Honey Mae."

"You need to go sit your drunk ass down and go to sleep." Her words were harsh.

This amplified his erotic desires and his obstinate demeanor. Ready to unleash her wrath, she turned her body so that she would be able to face her intoxicated husband. Vigorously she moved to loosen his grip, but moved deeper into his mighty hold.

"Let me go got damn it!" Now being able to smell the alcohol that reeked from his nostril as his breath fell heavy on her face.

"Let me go," she repeated.

"I'll let you go alright."

When she opened her mouth to speak, he planted his mouth over hers kissing her hard. She tried again to push him away. He only became stronger and more determined. When the kiss was done, he picked her up in his arms and carried her into their bedroom closing the door behind them.

Tossing her on the bed, she tried to get away. But he briskly grabbed her by her pants, almost pulling them off. Desperation was drawn over her face. She wanted to get away from his aggressive actions.

"Your ass has gone got damn crazy!" Still trying to crawl across the bed to the other side, she yelled to the top of her lungs. Oblivious to the fact that she may have awakened the children, but amazingly she didn't. She suddenly realized she might wake them, she lowered her voice.

"Mitch, you need to go and sit down before someone gets hurt."

He said quite impatient, "I'm your husband and you are my wife and remember till death due us part, bitch." His words were ice, colder than the Hudson River in February.

His eyes cut through her soul like a double edged razor, delivering a clue that there remained very little to retrieve in this lifeless relationship. She ended her struggle to get away. For the first time in her life, she felt the loss of control over any part of her world.

She lay there motionless as he began removing her clothes piece by piece. Inside, her emotions were racing, elevating her thoughts, making her all too well aware of what was actually happening.

Mitch had gained the authority as her powers diminished. Now having her entirely undressed, he took a couple of steps backwards to get the full view of her delicious and overwhelmingly beautiful nude brown body.

Expressing his appreciation, he whispered these words as to let no one else hear while regaining his footsteps, "God created a wonderful work of art when he created you."

Stretching out his hand, he began caressing her silky smooth skin. He unbuttoned his shirt exposing his well sculptured chest rippled with waves and waves of muscles. Unbuckling his belt to his trousers allowing them to fall freely to his ankles, he stepped out of them and removing his undergarments. He stood there visibly exposed.

He crawled unto the bed and kissed his wife once again. She didn't refuse him. This time when he kissed her it was not as hard and aggressive.

Kissing her cheeks, eyelids, nose and chin he let his hand glide down caressing each part of her body slowly. No longer was she able to just lie there pretending he had no effect. Her body started to move rhythmically to his every touch.

She whispered in his ear softly, "You bastard."

His kisses had traveled to her waist and then he inserted his tongue into her belly button and she shivered; boldly he turned her over onto her stomach rubbing his hands over her body. Unwillingly, she moaned with pleasure.

His hands were tender everywhere he touched. Frightened, she thought he would become rough and dangerously physical. Her breathing became rapid then he said, "You've always told me to kiss your ass, tonight I will."

He bit her hard on her behind. The pain was excruciating, her scream intense. Tears rolled down her face as she begged him to stop. Now Mitch's moaning of pleasure, was coming from biting her on the other cheek. He no longer desired to give good feelings toward her and at the same time her senses turned into hateful rage.

A surge of power gave her strength to say, "Get off me you son of a bitch!"

She wiggled and moving with all her might struggling to be free.

He said to her, "Shut up and enjoy," while attempting to cover her mouth to muzzle her screaming. That was his fatal mistake. She sank her teeth into his hand and held on causing him to yell out and roll from on top of her. That was when she released his hand from her mouth.

Feeling victorious, as she was getting up from the bed, she said, "You've lost the got damn mind your mama gave you; you're messing with the wrong black ass woman now. You'd better sit your black ass down like I said before or you can get ready to make a visit to your dead mama."

He was drunk but fully aware of the venomous words. Jumping up, he charged toward Honey Mae and found his bitten hand around her neck. Falling to the floor Mitch landed on top of her with his hand still attached to her neck.

She was gasping for air while trying to peel his hands away. He began taunting her, "Talk crap now, you stupid bitch."

His hands grew tighter. "I can't hear you." He said through clenched teeth.

She was squirming under his body, desperately trying for freedom.

"Moving like that I don't know what you want, to be released or for me to start loving on you again. Why don't you tell me because, I can't hear you."

Her eyes began to roll into the back of her head showing nothing but the white. This frightened Mitch. As he was releasing her, she began panting with deep breaths. He rolled off her onto his back and just lay there on the floor while she frantically fought for air. She massaged and kneaded her neck seeking to stimulate oxygen flow.

Regaining her composure she looked to her left to find a weeping Mitch. Sympathy was not available; instead hate and anger showed up. Turning her head to the right and without searching, she saw her spike stiletto come into view. Clutching it tightly she brought it forcefully across her body introducing the heel of the shoe to his skull.

Blood sprung from the wound like a geyser. This time it was his turn to groan loud; this time it was not with pleasure.

Gathering herself, she propped on her elbows and said, "Next time, you drunk son of a bitch, when somebody tells you to sit your drunk ass down, you will. But I guess now you'll have to lay down."

Proud she spat on him and got up, leaving him unconscious on the cold hard floor, kicking him as she walked away. She then went in to check on her children, giving no thought as to her husband possibly being dead or in need of medical assistance.

When she came back into the room to put on her bed clothes, she thrust a rack of clothes she had been drying by the fire, on top of him, closed the door and went back into her sons' room climbing into the twin bed with Bobby. That night she slept well.

CHAPTER 17

Morning came and the bright sunshine unveiled its first appearance for the day through the sheer window covering, placing itself on Mitch's blood soaked face and shirt. Wiping his head when he tried to move, he found the pain extreme. Feeling around his face, he located the lump; then looking at his hand, he saw the massive amount of blood.

He began to have total recall as to why the blood and lump existed. Pushing the pile of clothes off him, he began struggling to bring himself to his feet. Once on his feet, he stumbled to the mirror to inspect the casualty of war.

He gave a faint chuckle to himself and said, "I guess you lost and maybe you are a drunk son of a bitch."

His nose begin to follow the aroma seeping under the closed bedroom door causing him to go to the kitchen. Sitting at the kitchen table was Honey Mae. She was poised and pleased with arrogance, as she sat there with her legs crossed, reading the paper, smoking a cigarette and having a cup of coffee. He watched the steam from the cup and the smoke from the cigarette, float in front of her face as he listened to her say nothing.

Never once did she even look up. Staying attentive to her study of the Birmingham News, she peeled each sheet of the paper away after glancing at her desired articles.

When she finished she placed the pages precisely in their original order. Then creased them into a fold and placed the paper on the table. Meanwhile feeling dizzy but sober, Mitch reached out for the back of the chair to maintain his balance. Pulling out the chair, he flopped down carelessly, aimlessly and somewhat lifeless almost missing the target.

The smell of bacon, the hangover and the injury located on his skull caused Mitch to have a sick feeling come over him. His glands started secreting and his stomach began churning followed by nausea. He jumped up from the table and went into the bathroom and started throwing up. Honey treated him as if he were invisible.

When he came back, before him he noticed a place setting. Assuming it was for him, he respectfully ignored and declined, *"Probably laced with poison."* He thought to himself.

After a long period, they sat there with only silence speaking. A second time, he hurried to the bathroom and immediately found the commode. Over thirty minutes passed and the raging volcano inside him subsided. But while there he decided to take a bath and shave.

When he emerged, Honey was still sitting at the table. She was just holding the cup of coffee with both hands staring in one direction. She looked as if she were in a trance. How well did he know his wife; he knew she was ready for battle. However, he decided to disengage himself from further drama.

Being disappointed by his lack of interest, and his not wanting to talk about the unfortunate incident made her blood start to boil. She wanted him to say something, anything. But for him to say nothing, she found disheartening.

Dressed in a white robe and a bandage over his injury, Mitch retrieved a glass of water to help wash down the aspirins for his headache. Then he left and went into the bedroom. A few minutes later, he came back fully dressed and headed out the door.

No longer fighting back her words, she said in an unshaken voice, "Just remember whenever you come back in this house and you mess with me, I have a high heel shoe that matches the other saved just for you." She spoke with confidence.

Mitch opened the door and left, returning home late, just in time for bed.

Each morning he woke earlier and earlier abandoning the premise not to have any contact with his evil wife. The one-time history of a great love had now diminished and fallen into rubble and ruin. It was a far cry from their honeymoon night of bliss. Mitch was now fully aware of what his dear sister Hannah had tried to tell him so many times, that he was married to an unbreakable witch.

He found it easy to lose his way home and found it even easier to get deeper into the whiskey bottle. Soon after, many extramarital affairs joined in with his loose ways. People often asked him, *"Instead of drinking and staying away from home, why don't you just divorce her?"*

Never answering, he found it easier to walk away from the question, just as he did walking away from the broken hearts of the women that truly loved him. In the meantime, Honey Mae's drinking had increased also. Eventually their sons started partaking of the destructive habit.

However, people found it interesting that the more liquor she drank, the better she became at walking in three to four inch high heeled shoes. From community to community from shot houses to juke joints she walked, leaving

Daisy to constantly watch over her children and the addition of Queen, her dead sister Lucille's daughter. Jack was hurt to know that his daughter could possibly have a drinking problem, but was delighted to have so much time with his grandchildren. He believed this was God's way of giving him a second chance at being a father and mending the broken connection between him and Honey.

This however, didn't sway his daughter's thoughts of him. Nor did it deliver any hope of salvaging what was lost between the two of them. During the course of their parents living and partying, time passed rapidly and the boys had become men and Queen had become a woman, so much of a woman that she was with child.

*   *   *

After Queen's baby was born she found it even more difficult living and coping with her Aunt Honey and found herself clinging more to her Uncle Mitch, she loved and believed in him so much.

One day she decided to ask him if he would speak to Honey about keeping Eric while she went north to look for work. About a week later, Queen left for New York. Unintentionally she never returned for Eric. Honey adopted this idea immediately; she not only loved the child but she loved the way the child looked, curly hair and the skin color almost of a white man. For some reason she became obsessed with the lighter skin complexion. Although with reluctance, during some summer months, she allowed him to go visit Queen.

Mitch contributed Honey's behavior of loving the lighter skin complexion, to her new found employment. She had begun doing domestic jobs, taking care of white couples' homes and their children. However, one particular white couple, she stayed with the longest, had three children, two girls and one boy. They were the Mauler family. Fusing the children together, Honey rarely went to her job without Eric in tow. Allowed by her employers if she had no sitter, he would always be with her. She told them that if they had a problem with this arrangement that they shouldn't expect her to work. During this time and era of the fifties, speaking to white people in this manner was unheard of but she never missed a day of work.

Constantly staying overnight and going on family vacations, Eric was a part of the family. Honey found herself always working, always away from home. Leaving Mitch alone she gave him time to produce anger; Rage had become his companion. Now he had begun to wonder why he remained married to this inconsiderate person.

*   *   *

The year was 1956, one of the hottest days in July. The city was without rain; grass and flowers had begun drying and withering. On the other hand, no matter how hot, you could always hear laughter filling the air as children played underneath the trees.

The fragrance from the magnolia tree was apparent but the wind was not blowing. The large whirlwind fans circulated warm air and melted ice cubes in homemade lemonade.

Mitch had been in bed most of the day; he had not been feeling well for the past few days. He felt so bad he missed work, something he had never done before. His employer knew he had to be sick for him not to show up for his shift.

Jr. was in the United States Army, where he had been since graduating high school three years prior. However, he was almost at the end of his tour and anxious to return home and find a job.

Bobby on the other hand was wild, loving women, whiskey and gambling. Whether it was rolling dice or poker, he loved the thrill. Like his mother, he enjoyed life. He was handsome like his father. Unlike his father, Bobby wouldn't work. When he did, he didn't keep the job very long. Honey Mae had spoiled him rotten.

Finding ways to excuse her son, she would say things like, "But my baby can make clothes look good. He may not have money but he was sharper than a rat's turd sticking out on both ends."

Eric and Bobby were happy but life on the home front was just that, a front. Some of the classy lady's secrets were about to be revealed.

On this day, Mitch was feeling sicker than ever, so he got dressed, jumped into his new 1956 Buick and headed for the store to get something for an upset stomach. On his way there he glanced at a familiar body leaning into the window of a brand new Cadillac.

Quickly he turned into a side alley to avoid being spotted. His suspicions had become all too real. It was Honey Mae leaning into the car window of the man she worked for. She seemed to be kissing him with great passion.

After finishing her indiscretions, she stood straight and began ironing down her clothes with her hands. Gathering herself, she blew a kiss to the man as she headed toward her walk home, a walk from the bus stop where she would have been dropped off from her ride on public transportation. Mitch watched as her secret love drove off.

Shocked by what he had witnessed, he now knew who had been the missing piece of the puzzle. But the biggest question he had at that moment, *"where the hell was Eric? He was supposed to be with her."*

He rushed into the store and bought his medicine then without waiting he left his change with the store clerk then got back into his car and headed toward home. He saw her walking ahead as he slowed the car down to pick up his loving wife, so she wouldn't have to walk home from her hard day of work.

Almost leaping off the ground due to the sudden arrival of her husband, she was startled. After seeing him, suddenly she began looking around as if she was being watched.

Mitch asked, "What are you looking for? Were you expecting me or waiting on someone else?" His words were calm.

Avoiding answering his question, she asked her own, "What the hell are you doing here?" It was apparent that she was shaken by his unexpected presence because her words were angrily produced.

"I'm picking up my wife. Is that a crime?"

"Your wife? I haven't been your wife in years."

Inside, he was about to blow a gasket but he kept his composure, even through her arrogance was becoming too much for him to stay in control.

"Well wife of lost years, today you're my wife again. Get in and I'll drive you home."

Reluctantly, she slowly walked across the road and around the car to get in on the passenger side.

She began questioning him, "I thought you were sick in bed?"

"I was, but I feel much better now." He gave her a smile, one of the very few in years. She became nervous.

Questions started running through her mind, *"Does he know something? Jonathan had just pulled off, did he see him? Is this son of a bitch toying with me?"*

Soon her questions would be answered. By then they had arrived home and got out of the car.

"By the way Honey Mae, where is Eric?"

She was speechless, standing there all glamorous in her white dress with floral print and her famous gloves and purse but she couldn't say anything. She was dumbfounded.

Stumbling she said, "I took him over to Daisy's."

"When was this?"

"On my way to work this morning, he was crying and he wanted to go over there." She was worming her way deeper into her web of deception.

"And you let him have his way?"

Agitated she screamed, "Why all the got damn questions?"

"I want to know about and where Eric is, it's my right. So I can ask all the got damn questions I like." His even temperament had escaped and was replaced by loud and rude anger.

"I . . ." She began.

When she opened her mouth to say something else, he cut her off, "I, is right you bitch. You don't have Eric because you've been too busy working Jonathan Mauler, your boss."

"What?" Feeling like a trapped rat in a corner.

"What, my ass, you know exactly what I'm talking about."

She hurriedly tried to make her way into the house when she noticed Laura Lee, her nosy neighbor, standing on her porch watching. Pushing the door open, Honey Mae leaped inside with Mitch hot on her heels.

Yelling, "How long have you been screwing your boss?"

Laura's ears perked up.

Once inside, Honey continued to say nothing as she sat down in the chair. While she kicked off her high heels, he asked her again the same question and his face more tense.

"How long have you been screwing your boss?" This time the question came with less patience.

He crossed the room swiftly, approaching the place where she was sitting. With amazement, she quickly raised from her seat filled with fear. Backing away from him, she stumbled over the ottoman almost falling to the floor trying to make it to the next room.

Once in the room, she slammed the door and locked it behind her. Making her way over to the chest of drawers to retrieve her .38 caliber hand gun which she had bought after the one Mitch bought became missing.

Suddenly she heard a crash. Looking around to see what had happened only to discover Mitch had kicked the door off the hinges. He stood there like a madman. She picked up the gun and turned around quickly to shoot but Mitch threw his arm up batting her arms away, causing the bullet meant for him to land in the wall.

Knocking the gun free from her grip, he slapped her hard enough to fall flat on her behind. As she tried to crawl away, he stood over her and planted his foot on her back.

"Bitch, I asked you a damn question and I expect an answer." His voice so loud, Laura Lee could hear him through the closed window.

The sun was beaming and sizzling on Laura's body making her visit outside less satisfying but she stayed on the porch, repositioning herself often.

It was extremely hot outside and hot inside. Mitch had lost all thought of this discomfort, thinking only of disgust.

Honey was squirming to be released from under his heel that was sinking deeper and deeper into her back. He raised his foot enough for her to roll over onto her back, but replaced his foot onto her chest.

When she looked into his eyes, they were red. His nose was flaring and his face was drenched with sweat. She saw tears rolling down his face, the same hurt she saw the night she hit him with the spiked heel.

122

This time he had no sympathy as she lay there helpless. His emotions were stamped with unwavering hatred. Thoughts of murder grew stronger in his mind. Honey Mae was afraid.

"Please Mitch." She begged.

"Please what, bitch?"

"Please believe me when I say I'm sorry, I'm really sorry."

"Sorry about what? Sorry you got caught, sorry the bullet didn't get me or sorry I got my foot on your sorry ass?"

"I'm sorry for everything."

"You know what Honey, so am I. Sorry from the day I met you. Sorry about everything except my sons, Queen and Eric. But as for you, you can go straight to hell." Then he spit on her.

All of a sudden, out of nowhere the pressure from his foot onto her chest began to decrease; she thought he was having a change of heart when she noticed him clutching his head. Dropping to his knees, he slumped lifeless to the floor. Her fear grew even more. This coupled with great concern, she screamed.

The scream made Laura Lee think there would be great entertainment as she began thinking, *"I hope he kills the slut."*

Laura's hatred and envy kept her filled with jealousy against Honey; praying for the worst to happen because she loathed her just that much.

She heard the scream again, a loud shrieking cry; it was bone chilling. Laura jumped to her feet ran into the house and returned with her oldest daughter Julianne so she could come and listen. Julianne's reaction was to call the police.

Meanwhile, straddled across her husband's chest, Honey was shaking him trying to get him to respond to her call. "Wake up, don't you die on me!"

Crying profusely, mascara circles under her eyes, she resembled a raccoon. Desperately shaking his body wanting him to open his eyes and say something, she shouted at him; "Please, you son of a bitch, say something to me, anything!" Hitting him then collapsing onto his chest she wept.

A knock came on the door and without hesitation she eagerly ran to answer its call. When she opened the door, there stood two policemen. She began crying and screaming to them, "Help me, help me please!"

"How can we help you ma'am, what seems to be the problem?" Trying to make sense of her hysterics. "Calm down and tell us what is going on so we can help you."

"It's my husband."

"What about your husband?"

"He's lying helpless on the floor." Escorting them back to the room where Mitch lay unconscious. With their hands on their holstered guns, the officers followed behind her.

—

Honey began screaming, "Help him! Help him!"

One officer yelled, "Get her out of here, and call an ambulance!"

One police officer took her into the living room and called the ambulance. Within minutes, they could here the sirens screeching.

The volume was loud; once it came up on the yard it ceased. Two men in white uniforms jumped out of the ambulance, they were carrying a stretcher as they came into the house headed for the bedroom. Honey jumped up to follow them but the officer intervened by grabbing her arm.

He said, "Please, have a seat."

Obeying, she sat back down then pulled out a cigarette, lit it, and nervously pulled a long drawl. Noticeably her hands trembled. She finished the cigarette and was lighting a new one from the one she just smoked before putting it out.

Pressing the butt into the ashtray, she could hear her heart pounding. When she looked up at the front door, she saw Laura Lee and Julianne standing on the front porch. She gave her attention back to what was going on in her house, ignoring the both of them.

Soon the two men came out wheeling Mitch on the stretcher. She couldn't move. She could only watch as they took him out and put him in the ambulance. She shivered when she heard the loud blare of sirens, breaking her hypnotic state.

The policeman began speaking to her, "Ma'am the ambulance is taking your husband to Lloyd Noland hospital. Is there someone that can take you there to meet them?"

Honey heard them but didn't respond; she just sat there.

"Ma'am, will you be alright?" The officer asked.

At that moment Laura Lee and Julianne came on the inside and sat next to her. "We'll take care of her," Laura said.

"Thank you," he said, "and we hope she'll be okay. If you need us call the precinct."

Laura knew he was being polite by extending this graciousness but she also knew in her heart this was the end of the journey for them. Their job was done.

CHAPTER 18

Mitch died on that fateful July day being only 44 years of age.

Aunt Tomorrow said he died of three possible things that were going on in his body; "A stroke, too much whiskey or Honey Mae Jackson. Any of the three were lethal."

No one believed that his drinking contributed to his death and no one believed he was old enough for a stroke. But everyone was more comfortable and inclined to believe Honey Mae's evil ways and possible master plan was the reason behind his death. Nevertheless, these were unfounded accusations. But after hearing the rumors, she found it amusing and intriguing that she was the subject of so much debate.

Concluding her statement, Aunt Tomorrow said, "Honey got what she wanted, Mitch dead and her living off his money."

Financially he left her stable from his insurance, pension and savings. Partnered with her deciding not to quit working, her life seemed to be together however, emotionally, she was in shambles.

People soon realized, watching her unraveling behavior and withdrawal, she didn't represent the cold-hearted hard woman she had always displayed about her husband. But now seemed to have been just a ploy to divert attention from how much she really loved him.

Instead of a hard heart, she seemed to be a case of hardship. Some people still refused to give her a break even with the knowledge that she possibly loved Mitch.

After a few months, she regained her don't-give-a-damn attitude. She would say things like, "if people are going to think and decide their conclusions about me that'll be alright just as long as they keep their conclusions down so low I can't hear them. So, if they are going to think it, I'm going to show it."

Adding fuel to the nasty street gossip, she openly, in the black community resumed her relationship with her boss, Jonathan Mauler. She no longer tried to hide the relationship. Her affair with him, to her, was solely about being in a different tax bracket. Never once did the thought of love for him ever swim upstream.

Unlike her feelings with Mitch and how her feelings swam without exhaustion, there was no comparison. Honey Mae's life now revolved around several different men, calling them her toys.

There were two men in particular besides Jonathan Mauler. Their names were Prentice Giles and Harold McKinney. Honey liked everything about Harold, his distinguished looks, straight hair and his skin, a golden bronze, it was his natural skin color; he was part Indian.

Some of the blacks in the community did not accept him, causing her to remember how they mistreated her father for the same reason. Her feelings grew for him, but her drawback was him having eleven children.

Harold's wife died at an early age, only a few days after giving birth to their last son James. Jessica, Harold's wife, had had complications throughout the pregnancy and not being able to afford proper medical care, she died from an infection, leaving Harold a widower with eleven children.

Most of the time, it didn't matter the amount of children that Harold had, Honey seemed to welcome him often.

On the other hand, the other man that she cared for, but far less than she did for Harold, was deeply in love with her, his name was Prentice Giles and he carried a jealous streak running down his back so wide people could see it from a distance.

Honey Mae couldn't tolerate that emotion coming from him very well. But she loved the opening of his wallet.

I remember my grandmother telling me . . .

"As long as you're a woman there is no reason for you to behind or not able to pay your bills. As long as you can spread your legs, you have opened the vault to your bill payer. Listen here you ol' black ass girl, just realize that you are sitting on at least a million. And no man can ever come over my damn house to sit, eat or prop up his got damn feet and not pay. That would be a sad mistake."

She continued by telling me the story about a man name John . . .

"John came over one day with a bag of groceries and I invited him to come in and have a seat and a shot of whiskey; I thanked him for the gift of food and he said, 'Anything for a fine woman like you.'"

"Well if being fine will feed me, I hope to be eating for a long time."

"Yes lady, you keep a beautiful home. It's always so neat and clean, make a person feel comfortable. Make a person feel at home."

"I ignored this statement because I knew in my heart that there would not be another man living in this house but Bobby and Jr. I held on to my frustration by biting my tongue."

He said, "Honey Mae don't you think you need a new husband in here?"

"I need to cuss your black ass out for thinking such a stupid ass thing."

"Why? You can use a good man and I know you'll make your new husband happy."

By this time I turned around from the stove where I had been preparing dinner, holding the large spoon I was stirring with, pointing it in John's direction as it dripped liquid from its tip and said, "Listen you got damn stupid ass fool, I won't smell another damn breath every morning except for my own. So if you keep talking about coming the hell up in here, you stupid son of a bitch make this your last damn trip coming here. And if you understand English, shut the hell up."

He became quiet and sipped on his glass of liquor.

"I was fuming. He had pissed me off royally. When I finished cooking, I took down a plate, piling on a healthy amount of food and garnished it with fresh parsley and sliced tomatoes from my garden I had grown in the backyard. He had sat patiently waiting for the food to be prepared."

I placed the food in front of the empty chair where I was going to sit down to eat. This irritated him greatly.

Then in a demanding voice he asked, "Are you not going to fix me anything?"

"Hell No!" I bluntly stated and begun to eat my dinner.

"What do you mean hell no?"

"You heard my words and I'm sure you know what they mean, I'm not going to fix you a damn thing."

"But I bought all the damn groceries, so I want to eat."

"What did you bring it for, to eat up the damn profit? I'll be damned if that's so."

John reached over to snatch my food away while he said, "If I don't eat, you don't . . ."

Before he could finish his words, the stainless steel fork went down on the center of the back of his hand. I could hear bones cracking. He started yelling and I pulled the fork out of his hand; he cradled his hand to his chest like an injured puppy.

"Now, get your black ass out of my house before you're not able to."

I reached into the kitchen drawer. He thought I was going to pull out a knife to cut him; instead I pulled out the .38 caliber pistol. The only thing John could see was the gun being pointed at him and the fool standing behind it.

I thought he would pee in his clothes and I told him, "Get the hell out!"

He started walking slowly backwards to the door.

I guess he preferred looking at the bullet coming than feeling it hitting his behind.

I told him, "You're walking too slow; my food is getting cold so walk faster."

He said, "You are a low down dirty bitch."

"I'll be the last bitch you'll ever see if you don't hurry your black ass out of my house."

Once in the car he rolled down the window while I stood in the kitchen doorway. It was dark outside. I couldn't see him but I could still hear him. I knew he could see me because of the light shining from the kitchen.

He shouted, "I won't be back, you crazy heifer!"

I opened up the screen door and screamed, "And that would be too soon, so you better floor the gas pedal and get off my got damn property! Because the next sound you'll hear . . ." She fired the gun in the air.

He sped off yelling, "You need help you crazy bitch!"

I went back in, put the gun on the table and continued eating, talking to myself, *"I must be hungry or I put my foot in this food cause it sho' mo' good. Just think I almost threw this food out with his dumb ass."*

*   *   *

A year to the month of Mitch's death, a baby was born and Bobby was the father. Irresponsibility became his way and absent father became his name. I was born one night in July at the University Hillman Hospital. The corridor was dark and gothic; it was the basement of the hospital. This is where they took and left black women having babies. They would line them alongside the dingy walls like cattle, all crying in pain.

Some were given sheets to cover themselves, most didn't. My mother was a small framed woman, pretty as a picture. People nicknamed her Doll. However, on that night the white nurse cared nothing of her appearance or what they called her; she was mean and uncaring toward my mother.

She told her as my mother yelled out in labor pains, "Shut your mouth, you didn't scream like that when you were getting full of baby, so shut up."

The pain from the labor was intense, but the nurse's words cut deep taking the pain to a new level, a level of humiliation. Humiliation didn't stop there for her. After my birth, Bobby married a lady named, Sherry.

Bobby came to my mother one day to tell her of his marriage and how he still loved her but how he had fallen in love with someone else. Sherry was now living with him, Jr. and his mother. My mother was devastated with having a new baby but somehow she prevailed.

Later, she would say, "I'm glad it was her and not me that he married because life for Sherry was hell. Ms. Honey Mae treated her less than trash. She never allowed Sherry to eat until after they finished their meal. Sometimes Sherry would get home before everyone else and the house would be cold but she was not allowed to turn on the heat. I guess Sherry was cold one too many times because one day after she left work, she never went back to that house. Next thing I heard, she had moved north.

You know, that old Bobby tried to come back to court me. Even having you, there was no way."

However, my grandmother didn't discover my existence until I was almost one year old. One day while walking down the carline, dressed elegant as usual in a navy blue sundress trimmed in white, navy sandals and matching handbag, she ran into my Aunt Louise, my maternal grandfather's sister. Through conversation, but quite deliberate, she shared the news with Honey Mae that she had a grandchild.

As suspected, Honey Mae began cursing like a drunken sailor, "That got damn stupid fool that I named Bobby, I'm going to kick his ass when I see him. He thought he was in trouble with me when I threw that rope over the limb of that oak tree and was hanging his black ass, won't be nothing compared to what I have for him today."

"You tried to hang him?" Asked Aunt Louise.

"Yes the hell I did and I'll do it again."

"You crazy woman, he's a grown man."

"Not living at my house with me, driving the car his father left and can't hold on to a dime or a job."

"Well it's your own fault, you have those boys rotten and that's the kind of fruit you get when it's rotten, sorry."

Honey Mae looked at Aunt Louise with razor cutting eyes. But this had no effect on her. She was Honey Mae's soup cooler, her match. While growing up she kicked Honey Mae's behind many times before Honey Mae surrendered and they became the best of friends.

Aunt Louise continued to say, "Leave that man alone and go see that grandchild of yours, she's beautiful."

"Her?"

"Yes, it's a girl and she looks just like you. Now go and see that baby."

Honey Mae left Louise, walking vigorously in the blazing hot sun. The weather never seemed to bother Honey especially when she was on a mission.

Once she arrived at our home, I was told that I was walking around in just a diaper. When my grandmother came through the door, she knelt down to receive her new and only grandchild.

This struck my mother as odd and phony because of the indecent way she had treated Mitch Jr. and Virginia after learning they were going to have a child together. My mother remembered the story when . . .

Uncle Mitch and a lady named Virginia had a son together a few years before my birth, but the baby died after a few months from whooping cough.

The night the baby was born, my mother was there with a midwife. Not even Virginia's mother stuck around, and Uncle Mitch was nowhere to be found. My mother told me later that Uncle Mitch didn't want to be around, because Virginia's mother didn't like him and because she could be as mean as my grandmother.

Soon after the baby's death, my mother learned that Virginia's mother was forcing her to marry an older man she didn't love. When Uncle Mitch learned of this, he went straight to Virginia and asked for her hand in marriage. Her mother was there and answered the question for her. "Hell no and you can go home." She said in an aggressive and hateful tone.

"But I want to marry your daughter Ms. Hattie."

Virginia standing there, all she could do was cry because deep inside she wanted her mother to change her mind about this arranged marriage and allow her to marry Mitch Jr.

"I told you, she marrying someone else tomorrow."

"Well that means it's not too late for me and I promise I'll take good care of her."

Through her tears Virginia smiled because she was pleased with his response. Her love grew more.

"Well your promises are too late. Her new husband after tomorrow will be taking her back with him to Cleveland, Ohio."

Suddenly Mitch Jr. was weak at the knees.

"Besides, Mitch," she said, "you had all the opportunity in the world when she was pregnant with your baby, but you didn't make any promises then. And what comes to my mind is the night the baby was born you were no where to be found."

"And neither were you." Virginia thought, while she listened to her mother's ranting and tongue lashing.

"And the baby was born in the very room you're standing, and the only person besides the midwife was Doll, with her scary behind. When she saw the baby head pop out she ran out of here so fast that we didn't see her for a week. There Virginia was; all alone with a screaming child and no one seemed to care. The only thought on her mind was; Where was Mitch."

Hattie sat down to finish what she had to say, "Virginia is getting married to a good man tomorrow and nothing you say will change that. No nothing."

She slapped her hands on her knees and told Virginia, "See your company to the door and say your good byes." Hattie exited the room.

Mitch Jr. cried, went past Virginia walked outside and got into his car. She ran out the door behind yelling his name and begging him not to leave. He heard everything she had to say but never turned his attention from the dirt road he was about to travel down. He drove off leaving his true love behind him.

When Virginia turned around, her mother was in the doorway and said, "He's good at being gone," she vanished to the other room, leaving Virginia to watch the road that lead Mitch away.

Uncle Mitch Jr. never married or had any children nor did he ever leave home; he lived with my grandmother till his death.

Awakened from her thoughts, she heard my grandmother say while clapping her hands together and entertaining my little mind, "Come here baby, come to mama."

My mother's eyebrows arched and many frowns on her forehead as she tried to tolerate the things my grandmother was saying. She allowed her to continue because she didn't want to hear her loud and abrasive mouth.

Mother said I toddled over and she scooped me up into her arms and then said my grandmother had the nerve to ask her, "Why in the hell didn't you tell me I had a grandchild?"

"First of all, Ms. Honey Mae, Rheese is old enough to understand what you say, so choose your words wisely." Fearful of my grandmother, however, this time my mother stood up against her.

"I don't care what you say I cannot respect you as a mother for not telling me."

"Your son is the one you should be talking to not me. It was his responsibility to tell you. I did my part; I told my family.

Then your grandmother looked at me with piercing eyes, put you back on the floor, turned and left. Not even a good bye."

"Your grandmother didn't see you again until about four years later. That was when we attended your father's funeral."

That was my first and last remembrance of my father. My mother and everyone else told me that he died from food poisoning after eating at one of the downtown restaurants. Old liver and rice was the culprit.

After arriving home, a few hours later he became deathly ill. After he refused to go to the hospital they finally had to take him anyway. They rushed him to the same hospital where I was born. Ironically, this is where he died.

I remember it was a cold day when they buried my father because my grandmother had on a long black mink coat. I also remember sitting behind her and my mother constantly trying to keep me quiet. Her attempts failed most of the time, as my tiny hands clutched the back of the pew that was in front of me where my grandmother sat, she turned and gave my hands a gentle pat then she turned away and never looked back again.

After everyone marched out of the church and got into many big and fancy cars, my mother held my tiny hands as we walked toward home, leaving me to wonder why I couldn't go for a ride with all of the people. However, the young child, Eric, was kissed time after time on the forehead while sitting in her lap, drove away with her in the big, shiny black car.

Many years later, my mother told me that night she was so afraid, she slept between me and my brother, afraid of the dead.

As I grew older the understanding of the separation of my grandmother and me became more and more confusing. I couldn't understand her loving Eric more than me or the children she cared for in the home of the Mauler's.

I began noticing the one thing that set us apart, our skin color. Had my grandmother become color struck, as black people would refer to, when someone cares more for the lighter skin complexion? It was apparent to me, their lives were more important and everyday she displayed her love by her actions.

However, her life took a dramatic turn after the death of Bobby. Unable to deal with things in her life, she had a nervous breakdown. She could no longer work; she had become disabled. Now fifty, but still well preserved, drinking became her favorite pastime, never stopping until she was drunk.

It was believed her extreme behavior became uncontrollable and was triggered after losing her beloved child, producing yet another personality. This person seemed to inject even more deadly poison into my already strange grandmother.

Talk around town was, she had no worries concerning money. Jonathan Mauler took care of her as far as retirement and social security benefits. Bootlegging sales increased and visitation of gentleman callers with loaded pockets were still welcomed.

She would always say, "Men should have two bulges, a bulge in the back pocket where he kept his wallet and the bulge that made his zipper want to pop off his pants."

I remember walking down the street passing her house, I was around ten years old and it was summer again; the sun was ravenous and hungry as a wolf. We had all been playing softball in the ball field a few blocks from her house. Hot and thirsty, I wanted to go by and ask her for a cool drink. As I was passing, I could see her in the backyard under the big shade tree entertaining many people. I changed my mind because I felt as though if she didn't accept me by myself, she definitely wouldn't accept me with a large group of people.

I went home brokenhearted.

*　　*　　*

I had not seen my grandmother since that day and a few weeks had passed by. Summer was coming to a close and bringing the first day of school to a fast approach. I recalled we were sitting on the front porch, my mother, her three sisters and one of the neighbors.

I was playing jacks alone on the concrete when my mother said, "Here comes your drunk ass grandmother."

Looking up from tossing the small ball, I saw the lady approaching dressed in my favorite color, a powder blue dress. Coming closer I noticed slits on each side of the dress revealing short pants underneath, I remember thinking, *"how pretty."*

Her sandals and handbag were the same color and her shapely legs gave the exclamation point needed to complete a fabulous look. Beauty for her was untimely. Most women of her age looked old, head wrapped in ragged scarves, breasts sagging and most without teeth.

Even though her teeth had been surgically removed, however, they were replaced on the same day with dentures that were custom made by the best dentist that Jonathan Mauler's money could buy. For a long time no one even knew her teeth had been extracted except for her, Mr. Mauler and the dentist.

My grandmother's arrogance evolved to a new height once she saw us on the porch. With her head held high, she had no choice but to extend common courtesy and to acknowledge our presence. I believe in my heart during her drunken stupor, she turned down the wrong street.

She started climbing the stairs leading to our porch which were great in numbers, twelve to be exact. Stopping short of ten of them, she didn't come any further. She stood there with one leg propped on the step and one on the step below. She was poised with her arms crossed in front of her body, a cigarette between her fingers and the handbag strap lay in the crease of her forearm. She beckoned me with a hand gesture to come to her, causing the ashes from the cigarette to drop to the ground. Inside my small mind, I cursed because I didn't want to go. I gave great hesitation before I moved, glancing up to look at my mother as though asking permission, hoping she would say no but she smiled at me and nodded yes.

I climbed down the stairs and gave my grandmother a hug. She stayed a few minutes with general weather conversation and then she was gone.

I remember thinking, *"There she goes back to Eric and her white children."*

They were her life and she was their world. I now thank God for the life I did share with my Uncle Mitch. He was the only person from my father's side of the family that was a permanent fixture in my life. He wasn't always the best, but to me he was the greatest.

CHAPTER 19

After that day, I didn't see my grandmother for years but I continued to hear the stories of how she used to travel with Eric and her white folk bonding the two families together for a lifetime. The closest thing I had to a life with her was hearing of her life with others. I yearned many days for a relationship with her.

Some of the stories I heard about her life declined from admiration to being ashamed of her many wild ways. Like the story that my grandmother once told me about the night she had gone out to the bootlegger juke joint with a man they called Lucky. Even though she was a bootlegger herself, she did not mind patronizing the other locals.

Well, on that particular night Lucky wasn't so lucky; his luck almost ran out. The night had been filled with cigarette smoking, drinking, dancing and a whole lot of card playing. The three-room shot gun house was occupied to its capacity. No one's sweat was his own. Laughter, swearing and loving someone else's baby was the theme. Time had slipped into the wee hours of the morning and Honey Mae had grown tired and ready to leave.

She staggered over to her escort and expressed to him her desires. Leaning over, she whispered into his ear as he sat at the table playing cards, "I'm ready to go."

He pulled another draw from the cigarette that was flopping between his lips without removing it from his mouth. A thick puff of smoke traveled up his face causing him to tightly squeeze one eye.

Honey Mae sat down in the chair behind him for a few minutes, growing impatient. She repeated what she said, this time with more gusto, but she still whispered in his ear, "I'm ready to go home got damn it."

Lucky continued to slam cards down on the table, talking trash to the other players at the table, ashes falling from his cigarette and he totally ignored Honey

Mae's request. She was quite annoyed at having to repeat herself for the third time, still no response.

He continued with his fun. This time not whispering, but at the same time she did not yell, she said, "Three strikes on my team is out damn it and that was your third damn time," as she stood to her feet.

Finally he responded, "Sit your drunk ass back down and leave me the hell alone."

It wasn't so much as to what he had said to her but the chuckle after his statement infuriated her.

Instead of sitting down in her chair, she started walking toward the front door talking to herself. "Of all nights . . ." She then slammed the door behind her.

No one could really hear the door slam because of the loud music and talking. As usual she was well dressed accompanied by her famous three inch heels. She started her half mile walk home.

Once she was home she found Eric and Jr. fast asleep. Fumbling through her nightstand drawer in the dark with ease she found her .38 caliber pistol. Then said out loud, "Of all nights, to leave you at home," giving it a kiss.

Realizing she would make better time, she took off her high heels and put on her gardening shoes. Quickly changing her foot gear, she dashed out into the night and headed back to the smoke filled shot house.

Once there, she flung open the door where she found her date still enjoying playing his game of cards. When she opened the door wide, she gathered everyone's attention because she had the pistol stretched out leading the way like a lantern.

As she approached, she cleared the living room. Nothing was left but the record playing. The people in the next room gave the same reaction. As she entered the room where Lucky was, his back toward her. Everyone saw her but him. But oh how he heard her.

Putting the gun close to his ear, she cocked the pistol. The sound made it very obvious to him what was happening. As he slowly turned his head to view the familiar noise, his sight locked in on the barrel of the gun. She pressed the muzzle harder against his face.

The cigarette he was smoking plopped out of his mouth onto the table. Fright rushed through his entire body causing perspiration to bead and roll down his face, like rain water gliding down a window pane.

Throwing his hands up in the air, he imitated a surrender. There was no laughter, no trash talking, and no record playing. They knew Honey Mae and a pistol were serious business. The only sound that could be heard was her voice telling Lucky, "Listen, you black ass fool, when I tell you that I'm ready to go home, got damn it, that's what I mean, I'm ready to go home. Now get up off your got damn sorry ass and take me home."

She kept the gun pointed at Lucky endangering no one else and never once did she think someone would call for help. No one there was that stupid. Her focus was on one person and one person only, Lucky. Everyone in the juke joint knew without question to leave the situation between Honey and Lucky.

Almost falling from his chair, he tried to lean out of the way of the gun, but the more he moved away, the more she pressed the gun onto his flesh. Not being able to escape, he decided that maybe he could convince and talk her into putting the gun down.

"Baby, listen, you need to do something with that thing before it goes off and someone ends up getting hurt."

"You are a stupid ass, that's the whole point."

"Okay, okay, calm down." He said as his hands were still in surrender mode.

"I am calm because if I wasn't you'd be dead."

"Okay."

"Heard okay before, now get up!" She yelled while kicking him on the leg.

He cried out to the patrons of the establishment, "Someone call the police!"

Honey looked over at the phone on the wall and no one moved toward it. Seeing that his plea did not work, he became submissive. Slowly rising from the chair, he finally stood up. The slothfulness he displayed irritated her.

"It's been two minutes you son of a bitch, since I told you again that I was ready to go home and I can't figure out why in the hell we are still here. So if I say it again, I promise you I'll get home while you're on the way to the got damn morgue."

His steps became quick as he rushed toward the door with her close behind. When they arrived at his car, Lucky nervously opened the door on the passenger side. By this time the front yard was swarming with the mass of people watching to see what would happen.

"If you don't hurry and open that door, you won't have to worry about the key, but how to get the bullet out of your ass."

Miraculously the lock popped up. He opened the door to allow her to get in.

"Do you think my black ass is crazy? You get in first then slide your monkey ass over."

Following her instructions well, she climbed in behind him. Never once did she lower her protection. Hurriedly he drove her home.

Making him get out of the car at the same time, she rushed out of the passenger side making sure she kept control over the situation. Walking over to the driver side where he was standing, she pointed the gun in his face.

"The next time someone tells you that they're ready to go home, you get your got damn black ass up and take them you son of a bitch. Now get in your car and get the hell away from my house before I shoot you."

He jumped in his car and as he sped off she yelled, "I think I'll shoot you anyway." She fired a shot.

Driving fast because of fear, he ran into the ditch, wrecking his car in the process. Honey Mae could see that the car was not moving from its resting spot. She went into her house and went to bed.

The next morning the car was gone. She knew he had to have come and got it, but she said if someone had stolen it, she didn't give a good got damn.

When I heard this story, I cringed to think of her fearlessness and lawlessness and how little she cared what people thought or said. Never did I ever hear her say or wonder what was said behind her back because as she told me, "Whatever a man has to say, he proved to be a man if he said it to your face."

A hypocrite my grandmother wasn't. She cursed and swore at many, regardless of race, creed, gender. High office held no exemption from her callous manner. She told me about one of her white gentleman callers, who was a lawyer friend of Jonathan Mauler but much older.

I questioned my grandmother about her intimate relationship with Jonathan Mauler then having a physical relationship with his best friend. I wanted to know how she could be so cold and heartless. Her philosophy was, "If you kiss and tell you're doomed for hell. If Jonathan blinked to stay home and play husband the cup of sugar I gave to Richard won't be missed from the pounds I have in store."

She went on to say, "If you're going to lay, don't lay cheap."

For many years Richard had shown interest, always in conversation about her with Jonathan, causing him to swell with jealousy. Deep down Richard knew something was going on between Honey and Jonathan, but considered that as Peggy's problem, Jonathan's wife.

Eventually giving in to his curiosity, my grandmother shared her lusty tricks with the white lawyer—the same tricks that caused every other man to dance to her music. After being with him several times over the years, she had become bored with his time, money and substandard sexual performance.

For reasons even she didn't understand, like with all the other men in her life, she would become cold but they wouldn't go away. Each time he came over, she was determined this would be their last encounter. While sitting around the table laughing and talking, this being one of the only things he could do well, he could always make her laugh; however, she knew deep down, she didn't want to be bothered or touched by him, but soon they made their way to the bedroom.

Kissing and caressing things became heated for him while she only pretended. Before she knew it, they were undressed and under the covers when suddenly he excused himself and left the room.

She thought, *"Damn! He better not have the gall to be sick of me and walking out."*

Minutes passed and curiosity grew. Easing her way out of bed and putting on her robe, she began searching through the house for him. When she reached the living room, she found him standing close to the blazing fireplace with his back toward her. Creeping up behind him in silence to see what he was up to, she was appalled. He was standing there holding his penis against the heat from the flames.

Enraged, she began her infamous ranting. "What the hell are you doing?" She cried out.

He was unaware of her presence and her yell gave him the fright of his life. Stumbling over his words and at the same time trying to cover his nude body with his hands, he began, "I, I, . . ."

Dismissing his attempt to explain, she shouted, "What the hell are you doing and what are you trying to hide behind your hands you son of a bitch?"

In a pleading manner, he tried to explain, "I was warming myself up for you baby."

"Warming yourself up for me? I'm the got damn heater. Is this some sort of weird ass white man's failed performance trick?"

"No baby, I was . . ." Cutting off his words again.

"Got damn right you were. Get this damn handicapped, old, limp piece of meat out of here. I'm here to tell you, if my stuff don't give you enough damn heat to make that old rusty pole get stiff, all the damn logs on that fire and all the trees on earth won't help."

He hung his head in shame.

"Now you get out of here," As she began pushing him in the chest, he backed his way to the bedroom to get his clothes and other belongings. She followed, almost walking on his toes.

When they reached the bedroom, she was so close on him he was afraid to bend over to retrieve his items. Promptly, he gathered the courage and filled his arms with his clothes.

"Now take your sorry ass and get the hell out." Again she started shoving, pushing and guiding him to the front door, where he desperately started fumbling with the doorknob trying to open his way for escape.

Finally managing to get the door open, she pushed him outside naked. Noticing that he had dropped a few of his items, he asked if he could get them.

She said, "Hell no!" and began picking the items up and tossing them in his direction.

His pride was crushed. He started picking his things off the concrete porch; then he made his way to his car. She slammed the door with great force behind him and positioned herself with her back against it smiling.

She said, "Damn, if I had known it would be that easy, I would have thrown him out a long time ago."

She was upset with herself because she knew the free ticket to ride on his money train had ended. But during the course of throwing him out, she managed to keep, after falling out of his pocket, his wallet and she felt the night was not a total waste. She never returned the wallet and Richard never called or asked about his property.

CHAPTER 20

Seventeen and I was ready for my high school graduation; the day was filled with bright sunshine, fun and laughter. My friends and I were making plans for hanging out as our graduating class filed into the auditorium.

All the young ladies were in white dresses and the guys wore black pants and white shirts. The auditorium was hot even while the air conditioner roared. We were so excited in our cap and gowns that even the heat could not affect or take away from our enthusiasm. All of my family was there, everyone except my grandmother.

Just two years prior, Eric had graduated and my grandmother, the Maulers and even Queen, Eric's biological mother, showed up for his walk across the stage. My grandmother gave him a grand graduation party. Fancy embroidered invitations were sent out as well as verbal ones to over half the student body, including me.

Eric and I had become close in the latter years of our school days. I realized it wasn't his fault that he was in the situation of having a teenage mother that moved away leaving him to live with the person that happened to be my grandmother. I also realized he had nothing to do with the color of his skin or the texture of his hair. He was as innocent to circumstances as I had been.

I ask myself, *"Why had I been so angry with him all these years?"* Ashamed, I even went to him and told him I was sorry.

I didn't go to his event but I heard later that over half the school showed up, exceeding the maximum capacity limit even for outdoors. His party was a hit and was talked about all summer long. Unfortunately, he wasn't here to listen to any of the reviews. He had moved to New York with his mother and at no time did he ever return south. We lost contact and many years passed; however, we had a moment in yesterday.

Today, I am thankful we had the time we did in order for me to know what a great guy he was, which made him a pretty good cousin.

My grandmother may not have shown up but my Uncle Mitch came to my graduation. He bought my high school class ring, paid any school dues owed and he lifted my spirit and my admiration for him beyond any level of applause or thank yous that could ever be given.

He wanted nothing to hinder my special walk; he was proud. The day wasn't saluted in grand form like Eric, but to him I was important. My uncle exceeded the capacity of love for any one human being to have and it was all for me.

I remember the time when Uncle Mitch sat down and told me that there was once friction between him and my grandmother. The friction sent a surge of separating electricity that caused a pause in their mother-son relationship. Unfortunately, the electricity was me. He told me when he returned home from the graduation that he needed and had to ask her a question that his heart had desired answers to for many years.

Immediately upon entering the house, he couldn't hold it back any longer. "Madea?"

"What?" She responded, her adrenaline still secreting and rushing through her veins, angry because he had attended the graduation ceremony against her wishes.

It did not matter to him at that moment how she was feeling. Angered also, he asked his question, "Why is it that you've never taken time to spend with your granddaughter?"

"You spend enough time for the both of us damn it."

"Is it because of what people . . ."

Stopping him in mid sentence, "Are you listening to the sons of bitches of the world now?"

"No. You know what, I'm listening to you."

"Well listen on 'cause I don't want to talk about that black ass child. So leave me the hell alone damn it."

"But Madea, she's ours."

"That black ass monkey is yours, not mine."

Hurt but not shocked by her disrespect, he asked his next question, "Madea this is something I need to know, I really need to know? Is the rumor true that after Bobby died, you had your lawyer friend block Rheese from receiving his social security benefits?"

Blurting out the answer before she could control her tongue, "You got damn right," yelling at the top of her lungs, "'cause I don't believe she is Bobby's child no way."

"Well even if that's true, why did you let Eric receive benefits from my daddy, with the help of that same crooked lawyer and Eric is not my father's child?"

She started to walk away.

"I can't believe you Madea. You're wrong, just wrong."

"Who the hell do you think you're talking to? You're the one that's wrong and you've lost your mind with it. I'm still your mama and I'm just as old over you as the day you were born. So you can go somewhere else with this damn Rheese business and take it straight to hell." Fuming with anger, she stormed out of the house and sat in her favorite chair on the front porch.

Taking a pack of cigarettes from her pocket, she removed a cigarette, lit it, crossed her legs and finished the glass of whiskey she had been consuming when Uncle Mitch came home from the graduation.

After that day, he never tried or brought up a conversation concerning me. Unfortunately tragedy struck shortly after this incident between he and mama. I received a phone call that there had been a shooting, Uncle Mitch had been shot. One of the local boys that Uncle Mitch coached in baseball, shot him during practice. The young man had become angry because Uncle Mitch wouldn't allow him to be placed in the lineup.

Uncle Mitch thought and told the young man he wasn't ready. The young man left the ball field went home and came back shooting.

When I heard the news, I was devastated. I had lost my dad and I didn't want to lose the only connection I had to my father. He was in critical condition. For weeks tubes were connected to his seemingly lifeless body. Visiting the hospital was awkward, causing my appearances to be limited. I had no choice with mama always at his bedside. I still was not one of her favorite people.

Aunt Mabel and Carnell came down to visit and be to with mama for a couple of weeks, trying to make these times easier for her to endure. Aunt Mabel also helped me during my absence from the hospital by giving me daily reports. I thank God for Aunt Mabel, especially since she had only known me for a short period of time.

Eventually, Uncle Mitch recovered from his injuries and was home when Aunt Mabel and Carnell left to return to Detroit. This broke his spirit for coaching the game, something he loved as much as he loved me. However, there were some good things that developed from this almost fatal tragedy, Uncle Mitch started attending Sunday school and church services faithfully. He also encouraged his mother to attend with him.

Each Sunday, they were both suited down and dressed in matching colors. From head to toe they were well coordinated. She was always telling me her famous slogan, "We were sharper than rat turds sticking out at both ends."

It's kind of funny what God has to do for us to hear Him and get to know Him. Sometimes the methods have to be drastic in order for Him to get our attention. God made Uncle Mitch and me even closer. God did so much work through this situation.

Many times Uncle Mitch would say, "Maybe God will do the same thing for you and Madea." I cringed at the thought.

Meanwhile, here in the south it seemed as though the winters were shorter and the summers longer. Life was good; it was during the seventies when black people were working and living better than ever. We had fine homes with two car garages, nice automobiles and jobs were plentiful. We no longer had to just work in the kitchen and mop floors.

Blacks had become CEOs of companies, doctors, lawyers, judges; we were everywhere we thought we'd never be. Times truly had changed because my grandmother, as well as Uncle Mitch, no longer drank liquor. But most of all, my grandmother had settled down from partying ways walking from shot house to shot house or juke joint to juke joint.

She no longer sold liquor. She no longer broke hearts or played high stake poker. However, some things will never change, such as, her cursing, smoking, wearing four inch high heeled shoes or packing a .38 caliber pistol. She was known not to just talk but to show action as she made her walk.

People extended common courtesy to her through fear. No one gave her regards or honor due to respect of age or intellect but was given respect because of shameful ruthlessness. The older she got, the worse she became.

One day Uncle Mitch told me that God had answered his prayers; he could mention my name and Madea didn't get angry.

Feeling good about this he stated, "It's a start."

I said to him, "A start to what?"

"A start for you and Madea to become what was meant to be, grandmother and granddaughter."

I kissed him on his cheek, placed my head on his shoulder and told him, "You're a good man."

Shortly after, he told me a story that happened before I was born of how my grandfather Mitch had declared before his death that the house they lived in would belong to his sons. When Bobby passed away, his shares converted to me, Bobby's only living heir. Speaking inwardly, *the house that I couldn't visit belonged to me. Wow, that means my grandmother has nowhere to live and the house that she is living in belongs to me.*

As my uncle continued the story, he shattered my world as he told me of a fatal mistake he made. Convinced by mama's attorney Richard, that his father and brother now deceased and my being a child, it would be in the best interest to place another adult's name on all records and deeds and any other legal papers alongside his in case something were to happen to him. The other name he suggested was Honey Mae.

Explaining, this would keep the city from taking over through probate court. Uncle Mitch bought it, hook, line and sinker. I was edged out. He really had no idea of what he was signing or the magnitude of its effects.

This story made me love him deeper but for this underhandedness, I hated my grandmother just as much. After learning of this, going over to help care for him had become bittersweet. Seeing him was a joy and gave me great pleasure, but with her I found myself thinking and sometimes being wicked.

Like the time when she cooked dinner, the aromas filled the air, the smell of the food signaled how delicious the taste would be. I watched her take great patience with the preparations of the meal. After she finished cooking, she carefully placed a small portion on the beautiful china and carried it to Uncle Mitch's room.

Never eating at my grandmother's house I, suddenly with a burst of wicked spirit, went into the kitchen without her noticing me, grabbed the fork and plate she had placed on the table and began dipping food from her pot. I piled it on. Upon her return to the kitchen, there I was still preparing my meal and hoping I had succeeded in pissing her off.

She asked, "What do you think you're doing?"

"The same thing my uncle is doing, getting ready to eat." I said this with much enthusiasm and with a voice of authority as I thought, *"One thing for sure she couldn't even think about trying to beat my black behind now."*

"You didn't tell me, young lady, that you were eating. You never eat."

"Well today I'm hungry."

Standing there in her house dress, she was frustrated. Her frustrations gave me hope as I continued thinking, *"I'm in her house, in her kitchen and I have the control."* I wanted to tell her. *"Now you can sit your black ass down,"* but chose not to.

After standing there looking at me for a short period, she declared, "I didn't make enough for everybody to be eating."

"I'm sorry I thought you had already eaten." I was lying as I had just seen her finishing cooking. I coughed over my food without covering my mouth, added joy to my wicked and sassy way, as I controlled my tone and my words keeping them in the safety zone of respect.

Then I asked, "What will you eat?"

"I guess whatever is left in the got damn pot that hasn't been covered with germs from people coughing and spitting on it." She picked up a cigarette, lit it with a match and began smoking it.

She inhaled then released a big cloud of floating rings. As the smoke traveled across my face, I turned and looked at her.

"Why do you keep smoking? You know it's not good for you."

"A lot of things aren't good for me, but I put up with it anyway and if you don't like it you can get your black ass out of my got damn house."

Again I said to myself, *"Your house? This is my uncle's and my house."*

Then to annoy her even more, I asked out loud, "Why do you curse so much?"

"Because of black asses like you," she stated.

"Oh," was my only response.

I picked up my loaded plate from the table, feeling some satisfaction with each forkful knowing she didn't like it and went into the room with my uncle, joining him to finish my meal.

When I finished I gathered his and my plate, brought them into the kitchen, placed the dirty dishes in the sink with much food residue and went back into my uncle's room. I told him I was leaving. I gave him a kiss and left without another word.

Knowing the dirty dishes in the sink would cinch it for me and knowing this lazy action would cause her nerves to crawl, I laughed out loud and headed home.

Mama and I continued to butt heads but soon Uncle Mitch was well enough to take care of himself and I vacated the idea of visiting the premises. This time the decision of my not going to that house was of my own free will.

By the time Uncle Mitch was totally recovered, he had planned a trip to include, me, mama and my Aunt Joan. We loaded the car with our luggage and headed to Detroit to visit Aunt Mabel, Rochelle and Carnell, Aunt Mabel's children.

I didn't really want to go on the trip because I had met a new guy and we had hit it off, not to mention a long ride with mama. But for my Uncle, I sacrificed the romance and dealt with my grandmother.

Once we arrived in Detroit, Aunt Mabel greeted us as royalty with a home cooked meal and wonderful accommodations. She made us feel at home. Later that evening Aunt Joan was picked up by one of her friends that she attended high school with and had promised to spend time with the young lady named Samantha.

Samantha came inside and gave a short visit with Mama, Aunt Mabel and myself. Uncle Mitch and Carnell were upstairs asleep. Shortly after, Aunt Joan and Samantha bid their farewell and headed out the door.

Meanwhile, I went to make a phone call, leaving Aunt Mabel and Mama sitting around the table when mama pulled out her cigarettes. Aunt Mabel intervened by saying, "Sister,"

"Yes" Mama hurriedly responded.

"I don't have ashtrays in my house because we don't smoke and I don't allow others to smoke inside."

"What?" Mama sounding shocked.

"Well sister you know Carnell has health problems and so do I."

Steaming on the inside, mama listened calmly.

"So I knew you were coming and I know you smoke so I made you some ashtrays out of aluminum foil and I put a couple on the front porch and placed some on the back so you could freely smoke, cause I knew you had to have your cigarette."

Pushing the cigarette back into its pack, she slipped them into the pocket of what she was wearing, giving the excuse, "I'll go out when I really have to have one." Sarcasm was heavy in her voice.

Paying her tone no mind, Aunt Mabel merrily let the subject drop. No one knew the rage that brewed inside of mama, but I could feel the chill in the air. We had planned for our vacation to extend to ten days but it was cut short to four days. Mama claimed she was homesick and was ready to go. I was not disappointed; I was also ready.

The morning of our departure, Aunt Mabel and Carnell walked us to the car, gave us a kiss and waved goodbye. All was well, or so we thought, as we stopped to pick up Aunt Joan from her friend's home where we found her packed and ready to go. When we arrived at her friend's house and with the wonderful sounds of greetings and goodbyes, no one would have known the terror that lay in wait.

As we began our journey home, suddenly, the devil released all the hell he could inside that Buick. When out of nowhere mama said, "I'll never take my got damn black ass where I'm not wanted."

Our mouths dropped and questions jammed our circuits wondering what was going on.

Uncle Mitch said, "Are we missing something Madea?"

"Missing home, where I can live like I want to."

By now, everyone was totally confused.

So he continued his questions, "Did something happen that we don't know about?"

"Oh yeah, something happened alright. That ass named Mabel didn't want nobody doing nothing in her precious house. I couldn't even get out of the bed and have a cup of coffee with the intentions of going back to bed, but when I go back upstairs, she has already made up my got damn bed. She must have forgotten that I have a got damn house too and in my house I don't ever make up the bed. I just change the sheets when they are dirty and get right back in it and stay all day."

Interrupting her foul unkind words and trying to stay gentle, he said, "Madea, tee Mabel was good to us."

"Good to y'all 'cause she loved to put on false airs, but see I know her, she is the same ol' bitch."

"Madea, please don't?"

"Don't what? Tell the damn truth. She put me outside like a cat just because I want to smoke a cigarette. She can fool all those church asses with her $500 suits and hats but she can't fool my got damn ass."

When mama said these words, I agreed immediately with her and said to myself, *"You are a got damn ass."*

Continuing her spirited crusade, we remained silent. "I'll never take my black ass up there again to visit that heifer as long as I stay black."

The return trip home was a hostile environment. Mama's last words kept ringing in my ears and made no sense at all, as she spoke harshly about Aunt Mabel.

"She better stay in Detroit and keep that retarded son of hers up there too."

By this time they were dropping me off at my apartment. I told Uncle Mitch he didn't have to help me with my luggage; I was capable of handling them by myself. Before the car could come to a complete stop, I believe I had jumped out of the car with my luggage in hand.

Getting out safely, I stood in my apartment parking lot, waving goodbye and did not move until the Buick Electra 225 had disappeared from view. I was glad the trip was over for me but my poor uncle had to live with her everyday. Somehow I had believed this trip would have been good therapy for everyone since mama had not seen her sister since the funeral. Daisy and their father were killed in a fatal car accident. *"Then again,"* I said to myself, *"why would I expect mama to act any different than her past behavior with her sister, especially after finding out their father had left Mabel everything."*

Years passed and mama never spoke to her sister Mabel again. The ignorance of my grandmother didn't and couldn't stop the birthday, Christmas, Mother's Day or Easter cards from coming in from Aunt Mabel. She would open them all hoping to find money inside without reading the contents of the beautiful cards. Once she found there was no money, they immediately went to the wastebasket.

She was set on hating her only living sibling and she was successful, but she was only successful in hating herself. Meanwhile, the lives in Detroit didn't cease to keep on moving forward.

CHAPTER 21

Honey Mae was still keeping time with Jonathan Mauler even though their romance had faded into memories that could now only play tunes of years gone by. Both had grown old and their youth had slipped away. Honey Mae's revolving door of love for gentleman callers had lost its rotation and the men had lost their firm flotation.

Hair turned gray, eyes grown dim, hands worn and her stride became slower as the years passed, Honey Mae marched on to another period of existence. Time had caused the beauty to fold away like delicate antique lace placed inside a chest of hope.

Rearranging her life without permission or consent bringing pain and sometimes loneliness, time brought a new status even she couldn't shoot or kill. Time always has the victory.

Sometimes mama would tell me, "Even though I am old, if I die today or tomorrow the world won't owe me a damn thing because I lived my life and always remember what a life I lived."

Looking at her closely I could see how her skin had lost its elasticity and wrinkles the unwelcome guests, began forming their way into a valley of crevices. This brought to mind a story told to me by her of a relationship she had with a man named Prentice Giles.

Seeing each other often, they always had a date on Friday night, a date where they would eat fried fish and hot potatoes until they were satisfied. However, on one particular Friday night while in the midst of conversation and enjoying their meal, Uncle Mitch came in and mama asked him if he wanted some fish.

This statement of concern caused Prentice to become irritated with Honey's pacifying ways toward Mitch Jr. Especially offering the food he had bought.

He answered, "No, I'll be leaving right back out," and a few minutes later, he was gone.

After his departure, Prentice casually mentioned how mama treated Mitch Jr. like a baby, catering to his every need and not allowing him to be a man. Prentice finished by telling her grown-ass son needed his own place, somewhere he could cook, take care of himself and buy his own damn food. This would be the greatest mistake that Prentice could ever make in his lifetime.

Mama blew a gasket; non-visible steam came from her ears as she snorted and exhaled smoke. "You're barking up the wrong tree now and pissing on the wrong got damn trunk, you stupid fool. Get the hell out and don't you ever bring your ass over to my house again and you can keep in mind that Jr. belongs here. You are the only one that needs to go someplace and take care of yourself."

At this time mama's favorite neighbor, Ms. Laura Lee, was sitting on her porch in her nosy position. When Prentice came out on his crutches headed for his car, he turned around yelling, "Oh by the way, I'll keep in mind who belong here, a young lady named Rheese, your granddaughter. Remember she's your dead son's child."

Ms. Laura Lee was surprised by his comment; she thought he had lost his mind.

Prentice continued yelling, "She is someone you have mistreated and disowned all of her life telling people she is not Bobby's child. Got damn it, she looks just like him, so if you think she's ugly; look at yourself and your son. She had no choice about her skin color or how she looked, so you can't hold that against her. You need to go to God for that. Bitch you need to go to God anyway."

By now everyone was outside listening as the scene unfolded.

"Get off my property got damn it before it's more than a leg but your life you lose!"

She showed absolutely no utterance of remorse Prentice just looked at her and let go a sarcastic giggle; then he said, "You know what you stupid bitch, shoot me and even kill me but in the end I'll be a winner, I'll have what you never had and that's friends and family that love me. That's including my dark skin grandchildren. So take your ass inside your house and live the rest of your weak life."

Having no recourse, she did what she did best, threaten his life, and with bound determination, back up every word she spoke. She retreated into the house and he thought she was going to retrieve her pistol. He calmly got into his car.

When she came back outside he was gone. She sat down in her favorite glider to smoke a cigarette, ignoring Ms. Laura Lee, who was watching from her porch next door. Ms. Laura Lee began remembering once before when Honey Mae pulled her gun out to shoot Prentice . . .

He had come to visit without notice and found her already entertaining a gentleman friend and when she wouldn't open the door to allow him in he began acting like a madman. He was circling the house and beating on the windows and doors but she still would not let him inside. After a while, she became highly upset with his foolishness and went outside to ask him to leave.

When he wouldn't leave after several minutes of disagreement, she dashed back into the house and got her gun. When he saw the .38 in her hand, he tried to run. She shot him three times, twice in the leg and once in the behind leaving him on the ground to bleed to death.

Jonathan ran outside, he was the person whom she was keeping company. He saw the body lying face down on the ground. Frightened, he rushed back into the house and called the police. He gathered his things quickly and told her not to say anything as he left the scene.

When the police arrived and questioned mama, she decided to deny knowing anything. The officers and authorities then had to wait on the only person that could tell them what happened and that was Prentice himself.

When he did recover, what a story he had to tell them. The statement he gave was that he had come to visit Ms. Honey Mae Purify when someone yelled out his name from in the dark and shot him from behind as he was coming to visit.

The police never believed him. They tried and failed many times to get the truth. They didn't believe him because he was facing away from the house when he was shot. The case was eventually closed.

In my mind, the law had only given her the right to shoot and kill.

I remember another story of when she joined a social and savings club. "All the members were women, we had young and old. The young acted like old pussies and the old ones thought they still had one."

My grandmother complained and downgraded the members often, a trait over the years she was known for. Each meeting everyone brought a covered dish. She considered most of them as the worst housekeepers. She ate food only prepared by a few of the selected eleven members.

One member, one of the selected few, was always found gracious and kind by mama. After all business had been discussed and everyone was preparing to eat, there was a knock on the door. Everyone looking at the other, began to murmur around the room, "We're all present and accounted for, wonder who that could be?"

Maggie, the lady and hostess of the house, opened the door. Merrily, she began to say before being rudely interrupted by the lady in the doorway, "Yes, may I . . ."

"You got damn right you can help me. Get Sam to the door."

Maggie stood there motionless and speechless in her own home. When mama looked up and spotted this distasteful and unwarranted situation, she put her plate back down on the table. She lost her appetite for the meal that she thought had been the best she had ever eaten for the first time in their organized circle

The stranger shouted, "Don't just stand there looking stupid bitch, get Sam!"

Just about the time when Sam's wife was turning to follow the instructions of the woman in the door, mama made her way over seeking to assist. Maggie looked into her face with the .38 caliber at her side. Many years later, Maggie said she felt trapped, like she was in the middle of a Mexican standoff.

At that time Maggie didn't know what to do. When mama realized this, she instructed Maggie to step aside. She quickly obeyed. Mama assumed the role of the lady of the house and took control adding a new twist.

She said, "Bitch, you got Sam."

Everyone saw the change come over the lady's face, from aggressive to submissive. Her false power had begun to diminish, leaving her tone to follow suit.

Knowing each other, the lady said, "Honey Mae, I'm not talking to you," almost in a whisper.

Everyone knew the woman except Maggie. Maggie only knew of her. She was Sam's lover; her name was Tempres. However, Sam was Maggie's husband.

"But I'm talking to you, you crazy black stupid fool."

Tempres had not yet seen the gun that mama had eased behind her back, but she knew mama was famous for carrying a loaded weapon. Since she didn't see the gun, Tempres believed they were on even turf and gained courage to step over the threshold of the front door coming closer upon mama's face.

Mama considered this as a threat, planting her feet firmly on the floor slightly apart, ready for battle.

"Get Sam!" Tempres' tone elevated again.

"If you think your disrespectful ass is so bad and bold, come on in and get him your got damn self, bitch."

As voices yelled, Sam rushed to the front of the house at the end of the hallway. He stopped short of the living room where everything was taking place, but he could see every act.

Shirtless and half asleep he said, "What the hell is going on in here?"

Mama answered quickly for everyone, "Damn Sam, is that all you have, a got damn stupid question?"

Nothing else did he say.

Turning her attention back to Tempres, she said, "Listen bitch this is not my house but I think you should get the hell out before trouble really starts."

Tempress came back with even greater force of her words. "Like you said it's not your damn house, now move out of my way."

"You don't know me bitch to be giving me orders." Pulling the gun from behind her and pointing it in Tempres' face, she cocked the pistol by pulling down the hammer. "Now you move."

Hearing the clicking sound Tempres' legs became jello. Staggering three steps backward, she tried to save face by saying, "Honey you've lost your mind."

"That's the only thing you got right since you found enough nerve to come to this house tonight and oh yeah, you're right, I have lost my mind wasting time on a stupid ass like you."

Shifting her weight from one hip to the other and as Sam made a step in their direction without turning around, mama said, "Make another move Sam and I'll use one bullet for both you bastards."

His movement ceased. She then made one giant step which brought her closer into Tempres' face, placing the gun on her jaw, Tempres' dignity came out of her in the form of a stream of pee.

Boldness flowed with great ease from mama's lips, "Now on behalf of this house Tempres, I'll speak freely. Turn your black ass around and go back to where you came from, whether it be hell or under a rock. But you got to get your black ass out of here."

Scared stiff, shaking like a leaf and wet with urine, Tempres couldn't move. Mama gave her a little more incentive. As she pressed the gun harder against her jaw, she screamed, "Now bitch!"

Tempres turned then ran. She jumped into her car and sped off.

They all laughed. Discussing the episode; some made the story bigger and larger than it was but no one could reduce the reality of it.

Twenty minutes later, Sam came through the living room and left closing the door behind him. Mama asked Maggie could she go out and shoot him. Maggie began to cry, mama took that as a no and told her, "Don't waste your tears on that sorry ass."

"But I'm not you Honey. I love him; he's my husband and I've heard that woman has a child from him and I've never been able to give him one."

Cold and to the point mama said, "You may love him, but he's not your husband. If he were, he'd be here giving you comfort instead of going to locate where that bitch went. So consider yourself blessed that you didn't have his children because that's one less heartache for you to bear. And just because your got damn name is on the same certificate as his, it only gives you permission to use the same name. So save those tears when those old ass bones of yours are hurting like hell and you can't do nothing but cry."

Everyone laughed, even Maggie.

Sam didn't come home until a few days later and Maggie continued to treat him like a king.

Mama told me their names stayed on that certificate and they lived together as man and wife until the day he died. Tempres had memories and a child that took her through pure hell, but Maggie had finances to help keep her comfortable throughout her years.

CHAPTER 22

Mama never changed. She remained the same person, insulting and degrading but the people always found her stories amusing.

Eventually alienation occurred between her and the club members leaving room for no friendships even though she and Maggie would talk on the phone every now and then until Maggie passed away.

As days passed, time continued to change. Mama started to believe that her past was catching up with her when on every hand heartache came her way, especially when Daisy passed away, her only and true female friend.

Uncle Mitch was dying, one disease after another invaded his body; diabetes, high blood pressure and pancreatic cancer. Worst of all a hopeless spirit invaded his body. Dialysis had taken its toll. After five years of treatment and no transplant, there was nothing else the doctors could do, except make him comfortable.

Uncle Mitch's illnesses were ravenous, devouring his body rapidly. I cried daily. When he was hospitalized, I made the hospital my home also. I cultivated friendships with the medical staff. They knew I would leave his bedside to go home only for a quick shower, change of clothes and to check on my grandmother who was now under hospice care.

Life was demanding and I was married to a man that had no patience or consideration of the changes I was going through. Sometimes losing time of the day, but I gained pace with compassion, patience, love and great respect for my dying grandmother.

Each day, I watched my uncle step closer and closer to eternity, while at night listening to his screams of gross pain, I felt helpless. There was nothing I could do but sit and watch.

One night in September, it was hot and muggy, I knew within myself it would not be long before uncle Mitch's departure from life when at that same moment a call came on my cell phone and on the other end was my husband. He began with no hello and demanded that I come home.

He said, "You need to get some rest, good rest; you need to come home." He repeated the same thing over and over.

I told him, "I can't leave my uncle."

Soon through much pushing and being controlled, I gave in and went home. After leaving the hospital and before I could get ready for bed, at least an hour later, the phone rang and the voice on the other end was familiar. With he voice trembling, the nurse from the hospital, said, "Rheese?"

"Yes," I responded.

"This is Ginger," our relationship had brought us on a first name basis, "we need you to come back to the hospital."

"Why, what's wrong?" Even though deep inside I knew.

"We just need you to come back here as soon as possible."

"But I need you to tell me why."

There was a pregnant pause. Then Ginger spoke again, "I'm sorry to tell you, your uncle has expired."

Standing there with the phone in my hand, half dressed, I was frozen like an iceberg. I knew he would die soon, but I was disappointed because I was taken away from his bedside in his final hour.

He took his last breath and I was not there holding his hand. When I hung up the phone, I was fueled with anger and almost hatred for my so called husband. I disliked him more and more each day as I prepared for my uncle's funeral.

The day of the funeral, when he escorted me down the aisle behind the casket of my dead loved one, knowing he didn't care, I felt the need to scream. Already aggravated by other family matters, I felt like the weight of the world had become too heavy to bear.

I found out after the funeral while talking with Aunt Mabel that my grandmother was still not communicating with them. I found this so senseless. I also discovered mama no longer associated herself with the church, not even the pastor. I knew there was no way she was going to rethink her thoughts.

I made a special request to later speak with the pastor one on one and he agreed. A few days later we met. During the meeting, I was surprised at his response to my question. Greeting me kindly we shook hands and he offered me to take a seat. He sat down also.

His office was well decorated, walls displaying his achievements, his diplomas, coins and pictures of him and his family. I thought he must love himself because his office was all centered around one person, himself.

We began talking, "I came here to meet with you Reverend Burns to talk about my grandmother because she is a lost sheep."

Speaking with impatience he said, "Nobody in the church or outside of the church wants to be around Honey Mae because of her low down ways."

As he stood up from his chair, I stood also but little did I know that the meeting was coming to adjournment.

So I said quickly, "But you are her leader, you are the shepherd over the sheep. You have to go around her."

"She hasn't been under my watch for years."

"It doesn't matter. As her pastor, you will always be her shepherd, whether here or there. Besides she has been ill and she needs her church family."

"Nobody wants to visit your grandmother; she's too low down."

"Lowdown or not, she is still a member of your congregation and you are supposed to be there."

Changing his tone, once he realized I would not back down and trying to find the escape hatch from this conversation he replied, "I know you mean well. However, your grandmother is not a kind person, leaving no room for anyone to come into her heart, not even her pastor and from what I've heard, not even you."

I knew then that I was talking to a stone wall. So I extended my hand to shake his and said, "Thank you and have a good day."

I left the room of falsehood feeling empty, recalling the words of mama, *"When I die Rheese, you take me straight to my grave and let the trees and the grass be the witness to my death but you better not take me up there to lay in front of those church asses."*

I would become offended whenever she made that statement. Now after that visit, I tend to agree. I had heard all the acclamations that he had given my uncle during his funeral and what God had told him to say but now anything that he would tell me would fall on deaf ears.

Days after the service Aunt Mabel and her children left Birmingham with the same bankrupt efforts of reconciliation. When she left town sadness housed itself inside of me. Even my own home had become too difficult to live in. I was running daily from one home to another trying to take care of my family and mama.

Eventually, my husband decided to divorce me because he couldn't accept my caring for a woman that mistreated me all of my life. He told me that, "he could no longer bear watching me put myself through unnecessary hardship for that woman of hatred." But I would always tell him that, "I had to do what I thought was right and what I could live with in the end because in the end, if I didn't live with anyone else, I had to live with myself."

I moved in with my grandmother. Doctors had only given her six months to live, but she defied all odds. Her lungs had become corroded from the abuse of tobacco smoke over the years, developing a disease called emphysema. Doctors had only given her that short period but she lived two additional years. She lived to the ripe old age of 89.

During those last two years mama was a terror to all the nurses, social workers and the great people that gave assistance for her care. Even sick, mama was still the same person. She was filled with an abundant amount of decorative curse words of which she used freely.

She was a woman who spoke her mind, right or wrong but for some reason people loved her humor. Laughter seemed to illuminate the room when she shared the stories of her colorful and eventful life—stories I had heard many times. Never once did she tell them any different or with less passion, convincing me that her life was notorious and frightfully true.

However, on one occasion embarrassment rose inside one particular offended victim; there was no laughter. This person was her social worker that had become too curious about mama's business. She was looking in the drawers of her nightstand and when my grandmother took notice of this, she said, "You must be a white stupid nosy ass but not in my house. If you don't stay out of my got damn stuff, I'll blow your white hands off."

Scared stiff, she stood up straight as if she was ready to salute. She said, "I'm sorry, I wasn't trying to be nosy."

"I know you're sorry, but if you want to keep your narrow ass, you better stay out of my got damn business."

"I promise Ms. Purify that will never happen again. I was just checking to see if you may need something."

"I want your white ass to check this, you ask me first and I can tell you what I have and what the hell I need and I can do it better than your nosy ass or white hands could ever do it."

Then mama reached underneath her pillow, hands trembling as she pulled out her .38 caliber pistol and placed it on the nightstand where the social worker had been searching. Then she gave her a phony smile.

The social worker left that day rattled and needless to say, she never returned. The next time a social worker came to mama's house, it was a new person. My grandmother never turned her in to the company but we assumed the social worker left by, "self request."

Even when strength was no longer available and her last breath was drawing near and lights were not shining so bright at the end of the tunnel, mama was incorrigible. Soon I knew that someday, not so far in distance, she would be leaving me. Leaving this world filled with exciting and detailed information needed to be shared with the entire world. Also, she withheld information of things that I should know and that I should know alone.

I never had the knowledge of all her cooking secrets, never tapping into the knowledge of her famous cakes and pies that sing inside your mouth. Nor would I know how to make all the beautiful quilts that were made by hand. Most of all, other secrets I needed to know that she housed of her adventurous life among women and men, young or old, sometimes inflicting pain on those lives she touched.

My grandmother never thought that she was ever wrong but always right. Whatever decision she made on any situation even if wrong it was final, she always had to have the last word.

Whenever mama was awake and not too fatigued I pounced on the opportunity to ask about my history, tales of my father, grandfather, uncle and much more about her. I remember when mama told me the story about the time when she was hanging my father but just before the noose tightened, she spared his life. She did not forget to tell me that if she had killed him, I wouldn't be here today. For the first time in her own way, she acknowledged that I was Bobby's child.

Recalling the day of the possible hanging, she said, it was fall of that year and Mama had dressed and made her sons breakfast before sending them off to school. Merrily they left home, books slung over their shoulders bound by leather straps. In order to catch up with his long legged brother, Bobby often had to run. But after finding himself lagging behind, he stopped trying.

He always wanted to emulate the big brother he idolized, but on this day his desires were to be unlike him. He didn't want to go to school. Instead of running to catch up, Bobby had a dime in his pocket and he stopped at the corner store. Mitch Jr. did not notice that his brother was missing from the crowd. He had joined in conversation with his friends as they headed to school.

Inside of the store he bought himself some penny candy and cookies; then went on his way down the car line. Playing with a stick that he had found, he sat down on the tracks and started eating from his bag of goodies. Unknown to him, trouble was headed in his direction.

Busy with self entertainment and not looking up, he didn't notice the shapely figure approaching him.

Walking down the car line like a beacon of beauty in New York and glowing like the noonday sun, she bragged, "Chile I was looking good in that two piece suit made of hound's tooth tweed; my waist was cinched with a narrow patent leather belt and you know I had my signature pumps and matching handbag. I looked good. I was sha . . ."

Interrupting her sentence, I said, "I know, I know, sharper than a rat turd sticking out on both ends."

Lying in the bed, she looked over at me, smiled and winked playfully acknowledging and confirming without another word that I was right. I laughed out loud.

"But yes," as she continued her story, "he had his ol' sorry dusty ass sitting on the tracks and when he looked up, he almost pissed in his pants. He jumped up fumbling over words so I grabbed him by his neck and pushed and pulled his ass all the way home.

I didn't have to say another word. I just allowed his thoughts to beat him up before I got him to the house. But when I got home I took his black ass straight to the backyard, still holding on to his neck. I looked under the house and found what I needed, a rope.

I sat his behind down on the back step while I made a noose on one end of the rope and threw the other end over a large limb on the old oak tree. Then I called him to come over to where I was standing beneath the tree. At first, he didn't move, but without a word coming from my mouth, I placed my hand on my hip; he ran over so fast he almost passed me.

Standing there next to me, he started pleading, 'Please Madea, please don't kill me. I'll go to school.' And then I told him, 'I know you will'. I placed the noose around his neck, tightened it and then I began to pull. Slowly I pulled he began to scream and cry, dropping his bag of treats. His feet started lifting, bringing him to his tip toes like a ballerina.

Sweeping them back and forth against the hard dirt on the ground, I can remember like yesterday one of the first words I shouted at him, drowning out his screams, 'You go to school got damn it or die. No diploma, no life.' His little hands tried to set himself free from the tightened noose around his neck.

I repeated my words once again to him, making sure he understood. 'You go to school got damn it or die, no diploma, no life.' I lowered his feet back onto the ground because I could not understand the words he was trying to say. Finally, he got the words out. 'Yes ma'am I'll go to school the rest of my life.' I released the rope and he collapsed onto the dirt.

He sat there in the dirt trying to catch his breath. Voluntarily he added, 'I'll never miss school again even if I'm sick.' I allowed him to go inside and change his clothes so I could walk this little bastard to school. I promised him on the walk, 'I brought you into this world and I'll take you out and I'll have a talk with God later, explaining to Him why I had to do His job.'"

Quite interested, I asked my grandmother, "Did he ever shoot hookie again?"

She looked at me with a stare and I believe she gave me my answer. I just said, "Okay, I understand."

Shortly after telling me the story she drifted into sleep. Minutes seemed like hours because minutes were like gold. How precious they were, precious memories I wanted to charge full steam ahead just to hear more.

However, time would not permit. As I watched my grandmother lie in that hospital bed dying right before my eyes, I became sad. I began grieving for something that had not yet happened. Just a few days before I had asked my grandmother, "if she were tired and ready to go?" She nodded yes.

I then asked her, "Was she hanging on worried about me?" and again she nodded yes. Finally, I told her that I would be okay and I would acknowledge the request that she had been asking and had not yet done. I would ask the nurses not to give her any more medicine.

After discussing this with the nurses, they came back to me telling me that the doctors were all in agreement. Hospice was called in to a 24 hours round the clock service, to give her comfort and care.

Everything at that moment became real. I had not slept in almost two days, only cat napping in the chair next to her bed. The nurses began insisting that I get some sleep and that I would be no good for my grandmother if I didn't get rest. Obedient to their request, I went to bed.

After I had been asleep for about three hours, Beverly, the nurse, came into my room. Waking me, with a gentle voice, she whispered in my ear, "Rheese wake up."

She continued to say, "I'm sorry to awake you, but your grandmother is passing and I thought maybe you would like to be by her side."

Disoriented, I jumped out of the bed and dashed into her room without putting shoes on my feet. After I got into the room I sat down and placed my hand on top of hers and in the background Beverly said, "Talk to her, she can still hear your voice."

I began speaking, "Mama, I hope you know in your heart that I did all I could for you. And I do love you. Don't worry I'll be alright. You just go and take your rest. And when you get to . . ."

That is when Beverly interrupted me, "She can't hear you any longer. She just moved on, she has passed."

I laid my head on her chest and stretched my arms out around her body, I cried. After composing myself, I called my mother and my best friend to come over for support. I needed them to be there while they removed my grandmother's body from the house.

Surprisingly my mother walked me through the entire preparation even when we had to view the caskets. My mother has always had a fear of the dead, but for this she did not grow weak. I acknowledged my grandmother's wishes and took her straight from the funeral home to the grave and allowed the trees and the grass to be witnesses to her burial.

But a few people showed up to join in; there stood around the grave site, the Mauler family, all the nurses from the hospice group, my mother, my best friend and me. No one from her church came nor sent a flower. For that I know my grandmother smiled, knowing in her final hour she was not surrounded by church asses; also, I didn't take her to the church.

After the service, we went back to her home; there stood Rochelle. Her flight had come in late and she was alone. Aunt Mabel did not come to say her final goodbyes. Even in death, they remained separated. Even in death my grandmother and I remained separated by the words I desperately needed to hear her say to me, "I love you."

One thing I can say for sure was that my grandmother lived her life and what a life she lived. After everyone had gone home and I was finally alone, I remember my grandmother telling me that her favorite song was by an artist named Bobby Blue Bland and she had adopted it as her theme song. I listened to the words, ♫ "I've had my fun if I don't get well no more I say, I've had my fun, if I never get well no more. My head is feeling kind of funny and Lord I'm going down slow. Somebody write my mother and tell her the shape I'm in. Lord, somebody please write my mother and tell her the shape I'm in. Tell her to pray for me and forgive me for all my sins. If you see my father, tell him not to waste no tears. Lord 'cause I've been living so fast and reckless . . . ♫

As tears rolled down my face listening to mama's favorite song while looking at the picture on her obituary, it became too painful so I turned the stereo off and said out loud, "You sure had your life of fun and you didn't get well no more but I pray you're in a better place now, Mama, you tore my life, ripped my heart out, but you couldn't take my spirit because God smiled on me." Knowing this I prayed, "God I know You are the provider and healer, please give my grandmother a place in Your Kingdom and forgive her wicked ways. In Jesus' name I pray." Peacefully I grieved.